KILL FEE

Also by Gary Paulsen

NIGHT RITUALS

KILL FEE

A NOVEL BY

Gary Paulsen

DONALD I. FINE, INC.
New York

Library of Congress Cataloging-in-Publication Data
Paulsen, Gary.
Kill fee : a novel / by Gary Paulsen.
p. cm.
Sequel to: Night rituals.
ISBN 1-55611-203-3 (alk. paper)
I. Title.
PS3566.A834K5 1989
813.54—dc20 89-46037
CIP

PROLOGUE

THE BOY LAY in the bottom of a shallow ditch not far from a dirt road that serviced the sod farms south and east of Denver.

He was perhaps nine years old. His eyes were dark and enormous—great brown pools and his hair was thick and black and luxuriously curly, cut long so some of the curls hung down his neck several inches.

His skin was a flat white, so white that the tiny spray of freckles across his nose and cheek stood out in an unnaturally sharp contrast that made the skin look even more pale—almost translucent.

He was nude and the body looked as if it had been pummeled with large hammers. The damage was so extensive the body was misshapen, broken inside.

The boy was quite dead.

He had been dead, lying in the ditch for an unknown time, a long, lonely unknown time; long enough for the pool of blood beneath him on the dirt and grass to have coagulated into a gummy sludge.

Dead long enough for flies to find the smell and begin investigating the corners of the boy's mouth and eyes, to lay the packets of small white eggs which would become maggots.

Dead long enough for two migrant women who worked at the sod farms—Maria Tangenta and Carmelita Infantia—to have come along on their way to work and see the small form in the ditch. They had crossed themselves—both of them had seen much violence before coming north and knew that it did no good to speak about it—and had gone on to work, afraid that if they spoke of the body the immigration men would come and send them back to the cardboard-and-tin hovels they had called home in Mexico. So they had made the hex sign—the sign was meant to ward off evil, deep evil, the only true evil, soul evil—and they had gone on their way. Only that night in the small barracks where they stayed while waiting to work the next day on the sod would they speak of it and the foreman would overhear them and make them tell him so that he, also, would go to find the body which had been there so long.

Dead long enough for the calls to be made, the police to come and the teams to begin work. Men hovered callously over the body, made sounds of work, took dozens of pictures from all possible angles and elevations, swept with small brooms and vacuumed with small machines to find and save every conceivable possible bit of evidence; powdered and dusted and whiffed and sprayed and poked and touched and lifted and brushed and dug until not one spare inch of the surrounding earth or the boy's body held any mystery.

And finally he had been dead long enough to bring Tally.

CHAPTER ONE

TALLY JANRUS STOPPED at the edge of the area around the body, held at the crime-scene notice and sawhorses and nodded to a uniformed cop standing there. Inside the area detectives were working and one of them—a homicide detective named Mel Tyron—noticed him standing there and nodded to him.

"The press has arrived." His voice was only

slightly sarcastic. Like most police he hated the press. But Tally, who worked freelance in the Denver area, didn't exactly qualify as the press. Or anything else, for that matter.

It was once said of Tally Janrus that he had never been a virgin.

At anything.

To be sure the comment was made by a disgruntled journalist who said Tally had just beaten him out of a story unethically—if indeed there was an unethical way to win a story.

But the description held. Even his looks left no doubt that Tally had been up and down the river a few times.

Medium height, with scrubby unruly brown hair and a beefy neck and shoulders, Tally physically occupied space like an anvil. On his forehead a white scar went from left to right, giving his eyes a perpetual questioning look that was deceptively disarming. The scar was from a mortar fragment in Khe Sahn that had seared across his head and killed the man next to him, dropping both men in a pile of bloody meat. It was not clear to the medic whether either of them was alive and he didn't get Tally's head wound covered quickly enough to avoid getting dirt in it. The ensuing infection made the wound heal slowly and left the white scar.

There were other scars:

A pucker wound on his left bicep left by a .30

caliber carbine bullet fired by a Mexican Federale while on a sweep against insurgents. Actually the soldier was simply looking for something to gang rape with his friends—preferably, but not necessarily, a woman—and had taken exception to Tally's presence.

A short line across his left cheek which showed mostly when he was in the sun for a time came from a knife wielded by a hooker who—like the Mexican Federale—also took exception to his presence.

A slight limp left from a broken leg he received while covering a strike at a meat packing plant.

A place in his mind that only accidentally opened when he drank too much—which happened less and less as he got older—full of ". . . quiet horrors and balls of snakes," as he had tried to tell a counselor his wife had brought in who was unsuccessfully trying to save his marriage.

Tally jammed his hands into his pockets to keep from touching anything and stepped past the boundary markers. He immediately saw the boy's body, which had been hidden by the men working.

"Christ . . ."

"What?" Tyron wheeled, then saw Tally looking at the boy. "Oh. Yeah. It sucks."

"What a shit place." Tally looked around the ditch. "What a shit place to die."

"So there's a good one?" Tyron turned and said

something low to another homicide man, then turned back.

"Is it like the others?" Tally asked but the detective didn't answer. Instead he strode forward and guided Tally ahead of him out of the crime scene and into a cleared place away from the vehicles and men.

"What's up?" Tally squinted when the high fall sun hit his eyes. It was just after noon and the morning chill was fast being cooked off. It would get hot.

"I wanted to talk to you out here . . . away from things."

Tally waited.

Tyron lit a cigarette, drew deeply, exhaled. To the west, through the yellow haze of smog, stood the Rockies. There was snow on the peaks—September snow—and it made them look closer then normal. Tyron stared at them, thinking before he spoke.

Still Tally waited.

"You know I've been a cop for sixteen years, worked homicide for six, going on seven of them. I could hang on for four years and pull the fucking pin and walk. Get a goddamn cabin on a lake in Minnesota or some damn place and count bugs . . ."

And still Tally waited.

"I got an ex-wife and child support payments . . ." He sighed, took another drag on the cigarette and a look around them to make certain none of the other cops could hear. "It's the same as the other two." He nodded towards the dead boy. "The same M.O., all of it."

"You brought me out here to tell me that?"

"No. Let me finish. There's some shit even you don't know." He scratched a rash on the back of his hand. "We got three in Colorado. Two boys and one girl. All Latino, all between eight and ten years old, all nude and out in the country. All beat all to hell, just pounded to nothing. One up in the mountains."

"I know about them."

Tyron nodded. "No prints. No evidence except semen left in the bodies."

This time Tally nodded. "All in the space of two months."

"Almost three."

"All that I knew . . ."

"Do you know about the semen?"

"What do you mean?"

"Sometimes you can get something from semen —a blood type—and sometimes you can't. When a guy puts out information in his semen they call him a secreter."

"So is this guy a secreter?"

"Not exactly." Tyron waited while two men with a body bag went past them and down to the body. "The tests were all jumbled at first and they couldn't get a good reading."

"And now?"

"Now they've figured it out."

"So the guy is a secreter?"

"Four of them," Tyron threw his cigarette on the ground and twisted it out with his heel. "There are four secreters that we know about—and maybe two or three others that are there but don't show strong."

"Four?"

"Yeah." The homicide detective waited a moment, still looking at the mountains. "It's a fucking club."

Tally said nothing. He thought about his sister's daughter, a niece named Ellen. El, they called her. His sister lived in Illinois with a carpenter. Tally hadn't seen the girl for three years. She'd be seven, no eight, now. He didn't like his sister but the girl sent him a Christmas card every year. Usually something with a fat bear on it. He thought about the cards she sent and her hair, all blonde ringlets, and he thought about the boy lying dead in his own blood.

"There's more," Tyron said. "There are more than four—we just can't identify them. There might be three, four more on top of the ones we can see."

"In all the kids?"

Tyron nodded. "Always more than one, two men. We're not sure if they're the same men but it figures . . ."

"There is a rule in my job," Tally rubbed his

neck, hesitating. "Never turn down information—but I've got to ask—why are you telling me this? If I write it and a paper prints it and you catch these bastards it could jeopardize your case against them."

Tyron nodded. "More than one case has been blown by the press. That's why we hate you. . . ."

Tally smiled.

". . . but we've got our asses in a crack on this."

"How do you mean?"

The detective lighted another cigarette from the first, pulled deeply, thinking, ignored the question. "More important than the semen—what you also don't know is that there are other kids. Three so far in Arizona, two in Texas and three in California, a couple back east in Missouri—all with the same M.O.—all naked and beat to shit and left in the country. Sometimes in wild country."

Tally frowned. "Like I said, why are you telling me this?"

Tyron rubbed the back of his neck. True exhaustion, the kind that causes headaches and early, early age were showing on him. "I'll tell you—I'd rather take a fucking beating then ask you what I'm going to ask you."

Tally had known him for seven years, knew his wife before the divorce, knew he was seeing a younger woman, knew he was going to have a hair transplant if he could work it off on his insurance somehow—but he had never seen the detective this overwrought.

"So don't ask," Tally said.

Another drag. He thought, still ignoring Tally, then he coughed and cleared the smoke out of his throat. "I'm going to see that you get a copy of everything I've got—I want you to find out what in hell is going on with this case."

"You want me to solve this?"

"You heard right." His voice was abrupt, curt.

"Knowing I may write about it and blow any case you might make?"

He nodded.

"But Jesus man, why? You've got blood types, some evidence, you can get genetic codes from the semen—sooner or later you'll pop this thing . . ."

"I'm being transferred," Tyron interrupted. "They're taking me off this and putting me on those gang killings that happened last week on Colfax."

"Transferring you?"

"Look, we won't get anything done if you just keep repeating what I say."

"But goddammit, that doesn't make any sense unless . . ."

"Unless?" Tyron said.

"Unless somebody doesn't want there to be any progress on these killings."

"Unless," Tyron shrugged again. "I just got the word from the captain. Who in hell knows who pushed his buttons—the D.A., a judge, his fucking mother—what's the difference? It comes out the same, doesn't it? I'm off the case. Jarrenson is on it and the son of a bitch stays open."

"And that's where I come in."

"That's where you come in." Tyron nodded. "Because they're all over the country the feds have come in so you'll have to tiptoe around them but that's no big thing. They don't know anything I don't know. I'll give you everything I've got and you tell me what you find out and I take it from there."

"How about the story?"

"Anything you want. I just want you to hold off until it's settled."

"If it's settled."

"Right—if it's settled." Tyron threw his second cigarette down and killed it with his foot. "Is it a deal?"

"Deal." Tally nodded. "How can I go wrong?"

CHAPTER TWO

BILLEE (HE HAD a terrible time keeping people straight about his first name) Carstairs held the phone against his left ear with his shoulder and wiped a bit of scum out of the corner of his mouth with the fingernail of his left small finger. It was a move he had seen Rosalind Russell do in a film and he copied it well.

"Honest to god, Faron, it was *soooo* boring.

They did things at the party that went out in the sixties. At one point that silly shit Sturfer had three women come out dressed in leather and pee on a glass table. Can you imagine?" He laughed, a high giggle that ended in something near a wheeze. "I mean that is *sooo* passé—they were peeing on tables back in the fifties, for god's sake. At least the sixties."

He listened for awhile. The dining room he was standing in looked out over a canyon bisected by California Highway 101. Across the canyon there was a huge billboard that read:

UNIVERSAL STUDIOS

Beneath the lettering was a picture of a tour bus showing happy people touring the studios.

"Oh, I knooow," he said after a time. "Imagine Diana or Shelly blowing a four thousand dollar outfit to see somebody pee on a table."

Again he listened. Around the room were sculptures and on the walls hung abstract paintings. To the casual observer they seemed to be just forms, convex and concave, all in wild colors. There were dozens of them—oils and bas reliefs—all done obviously by the same artist, and all competently worked, if repetitious. It was only after a few moments' study that it became apparent they were all pornographic; that all of the convex curves fit into all the concave curves. The house, Billee once told a visitor, was decorated in early fellatio.

"Oh, I kn*ooowww,*" he said into the phone

again—a phrase he had copied effectively from Sybil Fawlty on "Fawlty Towers." "And don't you just know that silly bitch will get rave reviews for the party? Listen, I've got to go but why don't you come to our place this weekend? We're just going to schmooze around and see what happens. Oh yes, I kn*ooowww*. Bye."

He hung up and went into the kitchen where he made a perfect Bloody Mary (which he always called "bloodies") put a stalk of celery in it and sat at the table for a moment, sipping.

Billee Carstairs was past forty, pushing fifty, but looked like a tan, slightly wrinkled thirty-five. He did not smoke, ate red meat only once a week, practiced a mantra to stay serene, had actually been to a session with a man who actually and honestly had studied with Shirley MacLaine at least once and had decided at an early age to devote his entire life to a kind of sexual hedonism. Although he didn't exactly put it that way.

"I'm going to smoke and stroke until I die, darlings," he said at parties. Frequently.

AIDS had done something to curb his activities, if not his appetites, and he was largely very selective and practiced safe sex unless he knew the man well.

Or unless it was with a young boy.

When the drink was half done he set it on the table and opened an address book. When he found the number he wanted he took the receiver from the wall phone by the microwave and punched the numbers. It was long distance and he waited.

As he was waiting for the ring another man—young and muscular though bald on top—came walking out of a hallway that led back into the bedrooms. He was wearing only a tiny pair of violet briefs and his well-worked and well-muscled body shone with a layer of baby oil. His name was Todd Wells. He looked as if he had just risen from bed, his eyes sleepy, the lids half closed. It was how he looked all the time, and why Billee kept him.

Billee smiled at Todd. "Oh, you're up. I've already started on bloodies . . ."

He trailed off and turned into the phone. "Hello. This is me. I have another job for you . . ."

He waited a moment, listening. Todd picked up the Bloody Mary, licked the rim of the glass seductively and took a drink, smiling. When he leaned down to put the drink back on the table a long hank of hair—which he expertly combed over the bald middle top of his head—fell off to the side of his face.

"We don't give a little shitty *how* soon it is," Billee said into the receiver. His voice had a sudden edge to it. "You get paid a hell of a lot of money to deliver on time. If you can't do it we can get somebody else . . ."

Todd leaned down and nibbled on the back of

Billee's neck. Billee put his hand inside Todd's briefs.

"All right," he said into the phone. "That's better, lover. Oh, there are some changes. They want a blond this time so you probably can't use Tijuana." He listened briefly. Todd started to respond to the fondling and Billee pulled his hand away. "Quit bitching. They'll pay you fifteen hundred more this time but they want a blond. A blond boy. Yes, that's right, the same age. And we need delivery by Friday." He held the phone away from his ear as a blast of sound came out. "That's it, lover, by *Friday* or we find someone else. Call me when you score."

He hung up the phone and turned to Todd.

"Not yet. First we have to finish our bloodies and then I have to make some more calls." He patted Todd affectionately and pushed him gently away. "Now just take that thing into the other room while I finish work . . ."

Todd left, pouting, and Billee punched another number. Again it was long distance and he waited for the codes to go through. He was old enough so that it still amazed him how technology worked; he was calling the Boston area and it sounded the same as calling next door. All the way across the country.

"Hello," he said, when an answer clicked.

He cleaned the corner of his eye with the middle finger of his left hand—a delicate move he'd copied from Barbara Stanwyck—and wasted no time on formalities. He'd met the man he was speaking to only once but once was enough. He was huge, a bull of a man, and completely, absolutely, totally bad. A bad ass.

"Listen," he said after collecting his thoughts. "There's been a bit of a glitch on this end. Getting a blond boy is harder than we thought. I know you're already committed to your people but you have to realize how difficult it is."

He paused a beat, another beat of his finger on the table. "Well, really, it's just a matter of a few more dollars. Yes. We have to hire extra people to locate the product. I think six thousand extra should cover it . . ."

He waited. Outside a sparrow landed in a birdbath made of concave and convex forms. It fluffed and washed in a pool of water beneath the end of a perpetually pissing convex shape.

"The point is it's like any other business. If you want a special product in a hurry you're going to have to pay for it, and that's that." He grabbed a pencil and scribbled on a sticky-edge note pad. "Yes. Six thousand extra. That makes it thirty-one thousand—and the arrangements are the same. We deliver the product, broken in and ready to go, guaranteed. Delivery to you at the same place—the private strip in New Mexico."

He used his finger to depress the phone switch

and get a new dial tone, flipped the desk reminder to a new name and dialed again.

"Jimmers, it's Billee. How's your plane? Listen, I've got another job for you. From here out to that same strip in New Mexico. Probably on Friday. Hey, Jimmers, check this out—you get an extra grand. Right. Twenty-five hundred . . . I'll call in a day or two with details."

He hung up again and leaned back in the chair. He had been doodling on the pad in front of him while talking and he now circled the figure:

$23,500.00

"Net," he said. "Net, net, and net . . ."

He went to the sink and rinsed the glass before putting it in the dishwasher. Then he turned back towards the bedroom to where the waiting Todd was ready for him.

Todd was almost professionally stupid—Billee couldn't talk to him about anything even remotely thought-provoking or intellectual. But then he didn't expect Todd to think. Todd was a wolf in bed—just a wolf.

And that's why Billee kept him.

He hoped Todd was ready.

Making money always made him horny.

CHAPTER THREE

Davey Hascombs was pissed off to the max.

His best friend Cliff Hansen was being a big snot-shit kind of asshole person without any reason at all and Davey was really, really, *really* pissed off.

He stepped back on his skateboard, put weight on the rear and expertly flipped it up in the air and caught it as he came off the mall parking lot onto the sidewalk. He had ridden on the sidewalk in the mall before, but the mall rent-a-cop didn't like it and would confiscate his board if he got caught again.

He was heading for the arcade room. Earlier in the morning he had scored on his mother's purse for six dollars and eighty cents. There was a new game —the Vulcannon—that was so real it damm near made you wet your pants and he wanted to try it. That was why he was mad at Cliff. He'd stopped by his friend's house to pick him up and Cliff wouldn't come—said he had to mow the lawn.

"Jeeesus snot," he'd said to Cliff. "Blow the lawn. I've got bread and we can play partners on the Vulcannon—come on . . ."

But Cliff wouldn't come and that was the end of it. The problem was his goddamn parents, Davey thought—they loved him, for Jesus snot's sake. Gave him money whenever he needed it, took him to places—sometimes took Davey, too—and made it so Cliff didn't mind doing things for them. Ought to have parents like mine, he thought, couple of turds. Don't even know I'm around half the time.

He walked into the arcade with his skateboard beneath his arm. There were six boys waiting at the Vulcannon and he swore again. It's just a shit-snot shame I'm only nine, he thought—if I was older I'd kick all those boys in the ass and take the game over.

Probably be an hour at least before I can get to the game. He looked at the other video games, thought briefly of Space Defender, then shook his blond head. It was just turning into a snot-shit-Jesus goddamn day. Nothing was going right and he wasn't going to make it worse by peeing away his money on old Space Defender.

He'd wait.

Go over to the concrete ramp four blocks away and work on his airbornes. Last time he almost made it—came all the way over in a half-Rudy before he blew it and crashed in flames and busted his ass and damn near his board.

Check it out—then call Cliff when he came back to see if the Vulcannon was open. Cliff might be done with the lawn then—or at least be willing to skip out.

Yeah.

He made the mall parking lot. The hot, San Diego sun had cooked and softened the asphalt and the wheels on the skateboard sank in enough to slow the board. Davey kicked a couple of times to get to the concrete apron which was hard and had a slightly downward slope.

He picked up speed and whipped out onto the sidewalk. An older lady—gray hair back in a bun, stepped out in front of him and Davey had to take a quick, split-S evasive maneuver.

"Goddamn brat," the lady said, almost without feeling. Tuesdays she always went to the market to buy her weekly three cans of tuna and on any given

Tuesday she faced death and mayhem from skateboards and bicycles dozens of times on the sidewalks. She flipped Davey the bird, adjusted her grocery cart and moved on.

The sudden evasive maneuver made Davey run into a parked Ford Taurus. Davey ran a hand down the side of the silver gray car to keep his balance, finished the split-S and recovered cleanly without noticing there was a man sitting in the Taurus behind the wheel.

The man was about thirty years of age with a deep tan and a gold chain around his neck. His shirt was open to show a few blond chest hairs and an enormous coiffed head that made him look like a bad parody of an evangelical minister. For this reason and because he actually was an evangelical preacher who'd made his bones preaching in tents throughout the Midwest, the man's acquaintances called him Rev. He still preached in the southern tier of states through the summer when the sun made the tent hot and all the sweet young things who loved Jesus stripped down to tee shirts soaked in sweat to worship and gain religious fervor. With a little help from Rev, of course.

But that was changing fast. Preaching the Gospel and rubbing against all those ripe warm girls was turning from a calling to almost a part-time job.

And what had been his hobby, the young boys, was starting to pay more than Jesus. Of course he had to deal with that horrible little faggot, Billee. He didn't like that. But it was business and besides, it wouldn't last much longer. What Billee didn't know was that Rev had been expanding on his own—had his own market contacts opening up. Pretty soon he wouldn't need the little faggot at all. Pretty soon he would be running solo.

Halleluiah, he thought, it will all come to pass. In its own time, all in its own time.

He pulled out of the spot next to the curb, wheeled around in the mall parking lot and drove off after the boy on the skateboard. He had been going to scout the arcade for the next boy but Providence had provided—as it always did.

You had to heed the word of Providence and stay ready to act when it provided, even as his hero Jimmy Swaggart did.

And didn't, Rev thought, didn't old Jimmy pull out of all that nicely for an old country boy who liked a little action now and then?

Halleluiah.

He followed the boy, holding back a half block. Next to him on the seat was a new video game in a box.

His bait.

If the boy was heading home, so be it. Rev would go back to the arcade. But he didn't think that was the case.

No. The kid was going to play—he had that look

on him. As soon as he was well away from the mall and the crowds Rev would make his move.

All in good time. Everything came in God's own good time.

CHAPTER FOUR

TALLY DROVE LOOSELY out of the city, heading south down the highway towards Colorado Springs. His car was like him—a beat-up Jeep station wagon that looked rough on the outside but which he kept tuned almost to perfection. He knew nothing of engines or mechanics except how to swear when they didn't work. But he knew a mechanic who used to be in the armored corps who loved engines the way some men loved women and Tally let him do the Jeep once every three months whether he'd been driving it or not.

Consequently the Jeep ran like a fine Swiss watch and he loved to drive—just drive—and listen to the motor.

It had turned into a beautiful day. Hot, but with the crisp clearness of fall so that mountains looked close once he was out of the smog belt and he stayed over in the slow lane though the wagon easily qualified for the left side.

He had picked up the papers from Tyron late in the afternoon. Tyron had been almost insanely paranoid about meeting him with the papers. He insisted on meeting Tally with a driving drop, stopping four times while Tally followed to make sure there was no tail and finally handing him an accordion folder full of papers and photographs.

"I expect to see Deep Throat hiding somewhere near here," Tally said, leaning over his car window and taking the papers. "Or Nixon . . ." They were out by the Cherry Creek reservoir on a narrow gravel road where there was little traffic.

"I don't like the way this is going," Mel said. "Me getting taken off the case could mean that there is somebody big in this mess . . ."

"Or it could mean nothing."

Mel nodded. "But I'm a cop, remember. And all cops are paranoid. Watch the papers and don't let anybody—I mean *anybody*—know you have them . . ."

Tally had put the papers in the back seat of his Jeep without looking at them. Then he and Mel had separated and Tally had driven south out of town, headed generally towards the Springs but knowing that he was really going to Karen's.

Karen—Kari—Denton had come to him like a present that he didn't expect.

He shook his head now, remembering. His life was usually peaks and gorges. Highs that left him breathless and lows that made him want to die. He couldn't help it. It went with the turf—what a teacher had once told him was—". . . the journalism thing."

Shit.

That's what it was—shit. He'd seen a woman in Beirut killed while nursing a baby and the baby still alive trying to get milk from its dead mother and when he wrote about that, saw it and wrote about it the writing dragged him down so far that he thought he never wanted to see anything again. And he'd seen joy so sublime—a father finding that his only son was alive after a plane crash in New Jersey—a joy that made his heart sing and he had never been able to iron those highs and lows completely out, to stay even.

He still went from high to low and the end result was that he was impossible to live with. Impossible. He'd tried one marriage. She'd been blonde, that much he remembered, but he honest to God couldn't remember anything else about her appearance and had to think to make her name come up. Priscilla. Eastern money. She'd seen him at a conference after he'd been nominated for a Pulitzer—he didn't win, had never won—and they'd hit it off. Except that she didn't like *him* so much as what he represented—the excitement of the press. Travel. Parties. And when it came down to the nitty gritty and she saw what his job really was—goddam hard work all the goddam time dealing with people who were like gum stuck beneath the counters of life—she couldn't stand it and had gone on. Two months they'd been together, then she mailed him the divorce decree. No children. No money either way. Done and gone. True love.

And after that it had been moments of sweat when/if they came and no attachments other than his Jeep and his battered Olivetti typewriter. (He hated computers.) And motels and hotels and firefights and dirt and blood and shit.

Journalism.

He thought that was all he got. That's how it came to him. Sitting in an indescribably dirty hotel room in Chihuahua, Mexico, waiting to ride out with a troop train to look for insurgents, drinking tequila shooters with an infantry captain who had a silver-plated .45 automatic and a brain smaller than a walnut, sitting there getting stone drunk he thought that's all he was allowed to have. This, he thought, this life this way—stink, dirt and all—that's all he could have because (he reasoned) he must have done something really bad, really wrong and this was the penance.

And then had come Karen.

Kari.

Their meeting had been odd enough and he smiled remembering it now while he drove down the long curves leading into Castle Rock.

There had been a rumor of a major drug deal out on one of the many small airstrips in the prairie west of Colorado Springs, near a small town named Elbert—a wide spot in the road. Normally Tally wouldn't have gone with such a rumor—left it to the police. But he suspected there was a leak in the police department (which turned out to be true) and that if he told them they would blow it. He got his information from two sources and the second source convinced him to override his better judgment and he'd gone.

It was going to be a night drop and he had a crude map on a napkin from one of the bars on Colfax. To put the best face on it he was honestly mistaken and became disoriented.

To call it right, he thought, his smile widening, he couldn't find his ass with both hands. He'd driven around in the dark, wandered like a lost sheep until just before dawn. There had been low clouds so he couldn't see the stars or moon or mountains—nothing to orient himself by—and he'd driven on worse and worse, narrower and narrower roads until even his Jeep wagon was stopped.

He was in a corner of a fence with no gate, completely lost and he turned the Jeep around to head back on over his own tracks when he saw a horse and rider coming.

He stopped and got out of the Jeep, waiting, and Kari rode into his life.

She was—even in rough riding clothes and a denim jacket—almost classically beautiful; could have been a model. Straight nose, wide, clear brown eyes, smooth, clear complexion that obviously required no work and a slim, beautifully proportioned body.

She had a small-brim Stetson on and was riding an Appaloosa that seemed to hum with energy. She rode directly up to him and stopped eight or ten feet away. Close enough to see him, far enough to get away if need be.

"I'm lost," he said, shrugging. "Completely lost."

She nodded. "I would have guessed as much—unless you *want* to be in the south corner of my pasture, in which event you are exactly where you want to be."

Tally smiled. "I could think of worse places to

be." He stepped forward and held out his hand. "I'm Tally Janrus . . ."

"The writer."

"You know me?"

"I've read some of your stuff. The piece about child abuse in the *Post*—the special on running guns to the contras out of Denver." She studied him, still cool, appraising. "Which still doesn't explain what you're doing in my pasture."

He decided to tell her the truth—rare for a reporter. You could hint the truth, imply the truth, leave a smell of the truth, tease with the truth, allege the truth but you never actually *told* the truth. Until you wrote. Then you tried to always tell it but it didn't always work. Hell, it never worked. But on the spur of the moment he decided to be honest with her and told her why he was there, how sketchy the information had been and how he'd become lost during the night.

She laughed. "There are several airstrips around here but I don't think any of them have ever been used for drug drops." And then, after waiting and studying him and talking to him, then she introduced herself.

"I'm Karen Denton." She pointed to the east, towards where the sun was now starting to show. "Would you like to come to my place and have a cup of coffee? I'll get you back on the road from there."

She'd wheeled the horse and cantered off and

he'd followed in the Jeep, admiring the way she rode. There was something between her and the horse, some bond that made her move effortlessly with the animal while it ran and by the time they were at the ranch he knew he was in love with her.

What made it so astonishing to him was that it *was* astonishing. He was well past the schoolboy or romance business and had long ago quit listening to his hormones but there it was—he loved her. This from a man who had been convinced he would never feel healthy emotions again.

And hell, he thought, bouncing after her in the Jeep, he didn't even know her—nothing but a name and the way she looked and rode.

She had a small ranch—a hundred acres—that had once been a homestead that she'd fixed up. She bred and sold horses. She had twenty Appaloosa mares and one good stallion and was not getting rich but was making her light bill.

That's how she'd put it while they sat and drank coffee.

Making her light bill.

After drinking two cups of thick, black coffee with sugar—smoke-jumper coffee, a sergeant had once told him—she'd shown him around the place.

"The barn was here when the Cheyenne came through," she said. "Did you read *Cheyenne Autumn*?"

He nodded. "A hell of a book."

"A hell of a march they did. Through two armies and a whole bunch of drunks from Denver who wanted to kill them. They came through here, just over there," she pointed to a rise west of the barn, "and the people who lived here shot at them and they shot back. You can still see the bullet holes in the logs of the barn."

She showed him the holes in the massive logs that had been hewn to make the barn—logs brought from the mountains forty miles west—and touched the bullet holes with a kind of reverence.

"Do you live alone?" He asked.

She nodded. "I was married for a time in New York—it was like one of those Barbie and Ken things. Sweetness and light and then I found out he was shtupping everything in his office and we divorced. I was sick of the city and used my settlement money to come west."

They'd parted friends, or at least good acquaintances and a week had gone by with Tally thinking of her every single minute before he'd called her.

"Do you ever do anything in Denver?"

"As little as possible."

"I thought a movie or a play or dinner or something," Tally had said. He felt like it sounded lame and she laughed.

"You don't seem very sure of anything."

"I want to see you again."

"I'd like to see you, too."

"Well."

"Well." She laughed. "Why don't you bring me a rose and I'll cook a dinner and we can see where it goes from there."

So he'd brought her a dozen roses and they'd had steaks and that night without speaking of it, without any production, they'd gone to bed and made love as if they'd been doing it all their lives.

"I love you," he'd told her but she shook her head.

"Not that. Not now. Let's just see each other and let it be . . ."

Which is what they'd been doing now for almost two years. She resolutely refused to come into Denver or any other city and he went to visit her as often as he could. She was always receptive and they had a wonderful time together but she never went beyond that initial commitment, never said she loved him. And he didn't mind.

She was the one soft part of his life, the one place he could relax, rest. Sometimes, when it was bad and he'd seen things he wished he hadn't, he would go and sit by the barn in a kitchen chair with a cooler full of Dos Equis dark beer and drink beer and watch her train horses and not think.

She was incredibly good with horses. Even in his ignorance of them—he didn't ride, had no feelings for them at all except to think of them as big dogs that ate grass—he could see how good she was, how professional. When she worked them on the lunge line or broke them to ride her hands, her manner was sure and steady and the horses seemed to take from her, grow from her.

As he did.

He turned left now at Castle Rock and took the highway that led out to Elizabeth, then Kiowa and down to Elbert. She lived east of Elbert in a large basin called the Bijou Basin—it reminded him of parts of the Serengeti in Africa. A huge bowl, miles across, with pine trees and streams and small cliffs out in the middle of an infinity of flat, open, treeless prairie. Her ranch was on a rise and from her kitchen window she could see Pike's Peak—forty miles to the west—and he loved the drive down into the basin to see her. It always lifted him—the view, the reason for coming.

He drove with the window down and heard the meadowlarks singing from the fence posts as he passed and by the time he reached the road that cut off to Kari's ranch he had moved his mind away from the boy in the ditch and the file in the back seat of the Jeep.

CHAPTER FIVE

ANDY KLEINST LOOKED like something close to a fat ferret—if a ferret could be fat. He was short, heavy, bald with a perpetually sweaty face and neck and quick, cautious, nervous movements so that his eyes seemed to have moved past something before they saw it and he kept looking back at things. It was most disconcerting for someone trying to speak to him because he would look away and look back and repeat this movement so fast and so often that it nearly prompted stuttering in the viewer.

This movement made his job almost impossible because he spent a great deal of time talking to people. Or trying to talk to them.

Like Tally, Andy was a journalist—a reporter. And like Tally he worked independently—sometimes as a stringer for the *Denver Star,* more often just smelling out stories for the handiest buyer.

Any buyer.

He had entered the second level of the fourth estate—the level that didn't show. Andy was part of the murky river that ran through the media industry that never came to the public eye; a roiling, dark muck full of suppositions and innuendo, what Andy called the lower duodenum of the media tract.

"I work in shit," he said when he was drinking, which was often though he was seldom drunk. "The shit of the news. The real news. The true news."

Much, most—almost all—of what Andy did was unprintable. He worked by guessing, then selling the guess—and the key word was sell.

Andy sold news.

To whomever paid the most.

He had been doing the same work for twelve years and had something of a reputation—not a good one, but one that people understood. If Andy got on a story he would not let go—even if it wasn't true. There was still money to be made just by *think-*

ing it might be true because the vast majority of his annual income, which was in the low six figures, came by selling possibly true stories to the subject of the story.

Kill fees.

If he found that the son of an oil magnate had been involved in an automobile accident in which drugs were involved and strings had been pulled to get the boy off—as had happened—Andy would "write" the story and then approach the father to see if he wouldn't pay for the story instead of having Andy sell it to the press.

Kill fee.

Blackmail, of course—Andy did not kid himself on that point and, indeed, made no bones about it to others.

"It serves the same purpose as other investigative reporting," he would say, to any reporters or photographers who would listen to him in the dive known as the Donkey Dick where they congregated to drink and become blind. "People pay for doing something wrong, they usually stop doing it, and I make out in the end. It's a lot like being God."

Once in awhile he even wrote and sold a story—usually to one of the supermarket tabloid rags—but that was rare. More often he "sold" it to the focus of the story and he never went back. If he took money to kill the story he killed it, and he never called for seconds.

He had ethics.

Like now.

He was sitting in the office of a successful broker who had a daughter running wild in the mountains with a band that played at Aspen. All hair and grease and drugs—just like in the sixties. Nothing had changed. Everybody wanted to be Jim Morrison.

"I have ethics," Andy was saying to the broker, who had eyes on the statehouse. "When I heard about this I knew you would want to know."

The broker held a typewritten manuscript with some distaste, put it down. As well he should. His daughter had gang-banged the whole band while they took pictures. Andy had included only one of the pictures, not too revealing. "How much?"

"It's more a matter of responsibility than of getting the story out," Andy said, thinking fast. He'd come to the office thinking five grand, but this man looked worth more, looked like he'd pay more. Have to be flexible here, he thought.

"How much?" The broker repeated.

"I have expenses, stringers to pay, and they will be disappointed that the story didn't get printed. It's their work, after all." Which was not quite true. He'd already paid the "stringer," actually a road man for the band who needed the money for drugs and who took a flat five hundred and didn't give a shit if any story ever got published anywhere because he lived on what the band spilled.

"How much?"

"Seventy-five hundred should cover it. It's a little tight but. . . ."

"Is a personal check all right?"

"Of course." Andy mentally kicked himself. He could have gone to ten grand, the way the man took his checkbook out and started writing—he would have paid more. He'd have to watch it more closely in the future, push the money higher. Inflation. People were accepting more and more and he'd have to move with the market.

"Thank you," Andy said, standing to leave. But the broker watched him in silence, waited, and Andy left without any further speaking.

He had the money, which was the purpose of the visit. The broker had work to do.

And Andy had ethics.

In the street he looked at his watch. Ten in the morning. The shank of the day. A new sun overhead and he had seven plus in his pocket. He'd go to the bank and cash it—speed counted in these things—then have a good breakfast in a good restaurant. Eggs Benedict and a dry breakfast wine. He loved wine with breakfast.

Then he had a noon appointment.

A contact at the courthouse had left a message on his answering machine to get back to him and he'd called and made a noon appointment with the man's secretary, wondering what he wanted.

Money, probably. If there was one thing Andy believed in—and that, he thought, would about be it, one thing—it was greed. All people were greedy. It was a given fact in the physics of people and the knowledge had stood him in good stead.

Everybody wanted something. Usually money, sometimes sex—but money was almost always the reason people contacted him.

He looked at his watch again out of habit as he made it to his car.

Plenty of time for a good breakfast.

CHAPTER SIX

THE REV PARKED the car half a block from the concrete ramps. The boy had been moving along the sidewalk near the edge of a massive cement drainage conduit and he suddenly disappeared over the edge.

He stopped the engine and got out of the car. The old feeling came into his throat—the tingle. He got it when he was speaking of the Lord in the tents in the hot summer and he saw the women holding up their hands to receive the spirit and he knew one of them, one of them would be his private little paradise for the night. The tingle.

Here it was—he had done nothing wrong yet, and did not have to do anything wrong. Well, not wrong, but illegal. All he was at this point was a normal man walking across the street. The tingle was there and he knew he would do it, but nothing had happened yet.

When he came to the edge of the spillway he stopped and looked down.

Four boys with skateboards were riding the curved edges of the spillway, whipping up one side, turning, careening down and up the other side, turning . . .

As the Rev watched, the boy he had been following made a plummet down, up the other side of the spillway and went into the air where he turned, holding the board to his feet with one hand, and shot down again to come up right next to Rev.

"Looking good," Rev said to Davey Hascombs. "Looking really gooood."

Davey had landed on his feet with the board in his hand. He looked up cautiously. He knew that certain men hunted boys. Had heard about the old (and young) farts that worked the streets and tried to get boys into their cars.

But there seemed to be no threat here. The man

didn't move towards him, seemed relaxed and looked like a pure geek. He had hair about nine feet tall and a lot of white teeth when he smiled. He kind of looked like the geek who tried to sell Davey's folks aluminum siding or one of those asshole ministers on television.

"I'm working on my overs," Davey said. He stepped back on the board and dropped away again, down and back up, but a little farther down the spillway. Still not far from the Rev, but a little farther.

And the feeling was stronger now. The hitch in his breath. He'd still done nothing wrong, could still walk away. Or. Or.

"Maybe you can help me," Rev said, standing still, his hands down. It was no good if you scared them. If he ran or took off on his skateboard Rev couldn't possibly catch him. Two many beers and too many dinners of southern fried catfish and chicken for that. It worked better the other way anyway. They had to come to the car on their own, had to follow him and get close enough and out of sight of meddlers or it wouldn't work.

"How can I help you?" Davey was openly wary now. He'd heard enough stories. Besides, grown men didn't just stop and talk to nine-year-old boys without a reason. A bad reason.

Easy, Rev thought, be easy now. Don't scare the little shit. He turned slightly and started away to lessen the threat. "Oh, it's nothing. I work with Video Enterprises and we're looking for children to test our new video games. But I can wait and come to your school."

"What games?"

And that's it, Rev thought, exulting. I've got him. "There are several. What we do is I get your name and address and give you the game and the player and you take it home. Then I contact you later and you tell me what you think about it. It's just a simple survey."

Davey looked at him, openly skeptical. "You mean you're going to give me a video game?"

Rev smiled. "Well, after I get your name and address and phone number. I have to have your phone number too. Yes, then you get the game . . ."

"Right now?"

Rev nodded. "I have one in the car."

Davey looked back in the spillway. A small breeze lifted some of his hair and the blondness caught the sun and flashed golden. The other boys had moved on, following the natural tendency of the curving walls to fall down towards the ocean, which lay some miles away. He looked back to Rev—still wary. "Why don't you bring the game here?"

Rev appeared to think. "Well, I guess I could. It's in a big box though and might be hard for you to carry. I could give you a ride home if you'd like."

Davey moved away suddenly and Rev thought he'd blown it, pushed too hard.

"I don't get in the car," Davey said.

"Of course." Rev shrugged. "Look, why don't we just drop the whole thing? I'll come to your school next fall and find somebody to do the test." He turned to walk away once more.

"Wait—let me see the game."

And Rev turned to see Davey next to him, following him to the car.

"I'll just see what it is and then let you know, all right?"

"Fine." Rev walked slowly, not touching the boy. "That's just fine."

And it was, he thought—just fine. Everything was just fine.

CHAPTER SEVEN

TALLY OPENED HIS eyes to sunlight directly on his face through the lace curtains on the window.

It was perhaps six—too early for him to pop awake the way he had—and he put his arm out to find Kari already gone. She loved to be up early working her horses in the softness of morning. He rolled to a sitting position.

He loved the room, the way she'd done it. It was

like a small late nineteenth-century farm bedroom with a pitcher of water on the oak stand by the window and wallpaper with small flowers on it and an old brass bed and silence.

No, he thought. It wasn't silence. The window was open and there were sounds. Birds singing—meadowlarks and sparrows and robins—and insects humming against the screen. There wasn't an absence of sound so much as a correctness of sound. There weren't any traffic sounds or sirens or jets or people screaming at each other the way there were in the city.

He pulled his pants on—jeans. Always jeans. Even if he wore a white shirt and a tie with a jacket he still wore jeans. And not what he called pimp jeans—with the little designs or the tucked-in cuffs. Just plain jeans the way they had been done since Levi designed them for the miners.

He padded downstairs barefoot and shirtless and found the coffee, rubbing his shoulder. Wound ache. Once, in bed, Kari had asked about his scars and he'd said:

"War story, war story, war story . . ."

"Is that like blah, blah, blah?"

"Exactly."

"But they make me . . . curious."

So he told her, this bullet and that knife, this bar or that picket line or this firefight or that artillery barrage and when he was done she shook her head in wonder.

"How can you still be alive?"

He shrugged. "I don't know. Many, most of the men I worked with aren't . . ."

He drank the coffee slowly, getting the first-cup good taste and making it last, looking out the kitchen window over the table. He had never lived on a farm or ranch and yet it all seemed to promote nostalgia in him, which made no sense. There must be some genetic memory of living with the earth, he thought. He could look at a farmyard and feel the tugs of it, the desire to be out doing something, the memory of things he'd never had.

He finished the coffee, went upstairs and cleaned up and pulled on a tee shirt and tennis shoes and went back down. With his second cup he went outside and was surprised to see Kari standing by the corral in back of the barn, one booted foot hooked on the fence rail and resting her chin on her arms on the top rail, looking across the corral out to the pasture.

Normally she would be working the stock by now, maybe training yearlings on the lunge line. Or fixing something. She was always fixing something.

He stopped beside her, offered her some of his coffee but she shook her head.

Something was troubling her—she had a sad look on her face. The way she looked when one of her colts died. But he decided not to ask her about it and in the event didn't have to.

"I was going to do a little laundry and thought I'd see if you had anything to throw in the machine in your Jeep," she said. "When I opened the back I saw the file and it had come open and the papers had spread all over the place."

"And the pictures," he said.

"Ahh yes," she said, "and the pictures."

"I'm sorry . . ."

She waved it away. "I'm the one who should apologize. Your work is none of my business. I shouldn't have looked. But Jesus, Tal, Jesus—are there really people like that? Who will do that?"

He rubbed her neck, felt the stiffness, the anger. "Yes. More of them than anybody knows."

"I didn't read anything," she said. "I just saw the pictures of the children . . ."

"I haven't looked at the files yet. I just got them yesterday and put them in the car and came out here so I don't know what's in them."

"They're police files, Tal," she said. "Real police files. Or copies of them. Are you supposed to have them?"

He looked across the corral and said nothing. The morning sun was warming the grass in the pasture and made small waves as the moisture evaporated. A bird sang. One he had not heard before. He said nothing.

"I know we never talk about your work except when I read it—and yes, that's the way I want it."

He had started to protest and she stopped him.

"But I wonder if it's all that horrid—is that what you see and do all the time? If it is, if it's that kind of *Enquirer* shit I don't see how you can remain unaffected."

I don't, he thought. I don't remain unaffected. He thought of the boy lying in the ditch. How can you remain unaffected?

"It's not all like this," he said. "There are other stories. Other types of things to write about."

She looked sharply at him.

"A few . . . I . . ." He thought before speaking. He'd had this talk before. With his ex-wife. And had started to have it with Kari but had been putting it off because "talks" usually meant the end of things. She had never pried, just as he'd never really asked about her past. It didn't matter. Or hadn't mattered.

Now it mattered.

And he found himself in fear, a cold fear that started in his stomach and worked out and around him and left a bad taste in his mouth. Fear that he would lose her.

"Look," he said, putting his cup carefully on the top of a fencepost and gesturing with both hands. "I work, live, exist in a substratum of America—the place where nothing is fair, where nothing is honest, but the place where everything, *everything* gets done." He paused again, looking for words. "The people vote somebody in, he becomes crooked—always—and yet things get done. Money buys everything, anything, and things get done."

"I don't understand what you mean."

He rubbed his neck, knew he was saying it wrong. "The engine that drives this country, maybe the world, is criminal. Is by definition illegal. Watergate, the Iran-Contra business, under the table deals—every once in awhile they surface and you see what is really going on. But there is really much more of it than the public knows. Or cares about."

"I don't see what that has to do with pictures of molested and murdered children."

"I live in that world—that sub rosa world of the criminal engine that drives the world. That is where I work. I try to curb it, hold the son of a bitch down, and I usually—no, always—fail. But you keep chipping, that's all anybody can do. And part of that world is that I am exposed to other aspects of criminality—the hard edges. Like this. I can't tell you about it, or why I have the files, and I'm sorry you saw them but it's done . . ."

"But rare, Tal. Isn't is rare? For this kind of thing? There aren't that many people doing this kind of thing, are there?"

Her eyes were so clear, so clean. She did not

want this to be and he thought of lying to her but that would be worse, would serve nothing.

"Some time back *Hustler* magazine had to ask its readers to stop sending pictures of child pornography because they were swamped," Tally said. "That did not stop. Has not stopped. I had to go up into Canada recently for a story and in the customs office as you go across there is a wall covered with pictures of children who have been abducted. It reminded me of pictures I've seen of the notes pinned to bombed-out buildings during the Second World War—people looking for their families, lost ones. Or the messages on walls in Chile left by mothers looking for their children who have been disappeared . . ." Tally stopped. "The notes in Canada are all over the wall—little pictures with notes from the families. 'Hang on, Steven, we're looking for you,' or 'We love you and will never give up.' "

He stopped. She was crying and had turned away from him.

"I'm sorry. But this is different. This story is different or I wouldn't be able to work on it. There would be no point."

"What do you mean?"

"I mean nobody cares about the kids. Not really. Not long ago a priest in Minnesota was caught after having molested over seven hundred children —kept pictures of the kids, boys and girls, that he'd had and I decided to do a story on him. On all of it. Nobody would publish it."

"Why not?"

"One paper told me it was too common. They had stories on file of priests molesting kids that they hadn't even used yet."

"Jesus."

"Oh, yes, Jesus." He snorted. "I guess Jesus—but this one is different. There's some hidden thing in this one, some big and hidden thing that I want to find out about and write about."

She sighed. "It seems so strange—that what we did last night could become so perverted and make people do such things. Isn't that strange?"

He nodded but said nothing. They had made love the night before in the bedroom with the flowered wallpaper and taken their time and he had not thought once about his life, the files in the car, Mel Tyron—none of it. Only the hot-sweet intensity of the lovemaking. But when they were done, while she went to sleep, he had lain and wondered if he could stop it, stop all that he had become and just move onto the ranch with her and help her with the horses and write books. He had a novel, maybe two of them, in a box somewhere. He knew some people in New York. He could keep from starving. He could write about what he'd seen, what he'd done and learned. He could just sit in the sun and hammer on his Olivetti. Then he'd gone to sleep and it had all gone away from him until now.

Just now.

He thought of it now as she walked away from him and went to the tack shed on the end of the barn to get the lunge line and start working the yearlings, thought hard on it.

CHAPTER EIGHT

MARTIN FLORES WAS very old—so old that even he did not know how many years he had; more than all of his friends who had died. More than all of the women he had known who had died. More than all the beans he had grown and eaten that had died. More than anybody he knew, Martin Flores was old.

And stupid.

I must be stupid, he thought, to be in this place

waiting for what I am waiting for—stupid when I should have wisdom.

North of the town of Espanola, which was northeast of Santa Fe, near some low sand and rock hills in the high desert, Martin waited.

He was waiting for two airplanes.

He was waiting to get rich.

He had an old tarp and had set it up beneath an overhanging rock face so that it would be nearly invisible from above and had been sitting, camping, as he had camped for years with the sheep when he took them into the mountains, waiting.

The planes had come twice to the old dirt airstrip near the river that he knew about and he had watched from a distance as men took a large, wrapped bundle from one plane and put it in the other and he knew it was drugs.

He knew drugs well from the sixties when the hippies were everywhere and there was much drugs and everybody was mad with it. Then there was not such money as there was now but there was some and he knew that drugs meant money.

It was not that Martin Flores was greedy. Not even a small amount. But he had problems with his joints now that the doctors wanted money to fix and to give him drugs—a different kind of drugs—to make the pain less. He had been using aspirin but now his ears whistled and he shit blood and so he needed the doctor's drugs and for that he needed money.

And drugs meant money.

They were bringing drugs in with the planes and they were sending money out and he thought at first that he could take his rifle and shoot the planes and take the money and move back into the desert and nobody would know. Shoot the men and the planes.

But there had been two men in one plane and one man in the other plane and it would have been hard to shoot all three men. He could shoot one or perhaps even two of them with his Springfield but even working the bolt fast he could not hope to shoot four of them. He had shot two men once when he was a young man. One of them he killed but the other one he only shot a little bit in the leg and the arm but they did not have airplanes and probably expensive guns and besides, that was when his hands were young and he could work the bolt on the Springfield with ease.

Now his hands looked like knotted rope and it was very hard to do things fast.

He could watch sheep and shoot coyotes but that was all that he was still allowed to do with his body.

He thought of the times when he was young when there were many things he could do; of the women he'd known and who had left him and how they looked when the sun caught their black hair or the skin of their back and he wondered how it was he could get old. How could anyone get old?

Why did not God keep you young until you died? Why was it necessary to age and become bent and have pain and not know even moments of relief?

He shook his head. Wasted thoughts on wasted dreams and wasted times.

All that counted now was the coming of the planes. He had that to do and that was all he had to do. When the planes came he would write the numbers of them and he would get a reward for telling Benny Rodriguez who was the deputy sheriff about the numbers.

That was how it worked now. You did not have to shoot men now, you just had to know their numbers and then Benny would tell the numbers to the people in Washington and Martin Flores would get a reward.

He did not know how much but he knew that it would be big. He had been drinking a beer with Benny in the cantina and asked how big the reward was when one gave the numbers for airplanes carrying drugs.

"More money than you've ever had, you old fart," Benny had answered. And though he was a little drunk and had his hand under the dress of Natina Lopez, Martin believed him.

Of course if the planes came and each only had one man he could still use the Springfield and shoot them. He could probably shoot two of them. And he liked the idea of shooting them. He had not shot anybody since he was young.

And so he waited.

Sitting under the tarp with a gallon jug of water and another gallon jug of red wine and some jerky and a pack of the little cupcakes with the face of the girl he waited.

The planes would come.

CHAPTER NINE

JAMES VACHON STUDIED himself in the mirror on the back of the sunvisor in the limo and liked—no, he thought, smiling, not liked, *loved* what he saw.

Twenty-eight, blue eyes, blond hair—somebody told him he looked like a tough version of an actor from the early sixties named Tab Hunter.

A tough Tab. He had not known who the actor

was—it was before his time—but he found a video of an old movie and watched him and there was some similarity. The same hair style, same innocent look although in James's case it was entirely misleading.

I, James thought, flicking the visor back up, am long past innocent.

The truth was he probably would have been dead by now if he hadn't run into Mr. Rissden. Raised in an orphanage in Pennsylvania he had been in and out of minimum security establishments until he became old enough for prison. He had a real talent for stealing cars—could pop a door and drive away in twenty seconds or less—and by the time he was nineteen he was making a grand a day when he worked. He sold the cars to a chop shop in the basement of an old warehouse—drive a car in and the man peeled the money off.

Until he got caught.

None of his priors counted because he had been a juvenile but the judge knew—James could see it in his goddam eyes—and the judge waxed his ass for him.

His first fall he took one-to-fifteen for grand theft auto and he was too pretty—way too pretty. He hadn't been in prison a week and some big bastard named Jackson "adopted" him. Jackson was a lifer who had killed two women for fun and even the guards didn't fuck with him and he ran the tier. In two days James had moved into Jackson's cell with him and nobody, but *nobody* bothered him his entire stay in the joint.

Except Jackson, of course.

Jackson still wrote to him but he never answered.

The problem was he'd started to like it. Not just the sack time—although that was fun too. He liked all of it. Being taken care of by a man, owned by a man, controlled by a man.

So when he got out he started doing cars again and would probably have gone down again except that he tried to steal Mr. Rissden's limo.

Big mistake.

James had seen the limo in an underground parking lot in downtown Boston. He scouted the lots. And the chop shop owner had told him he'd pay a grand for a limo.

A grand. For one hop, a grand.

Which was worth a lot of nose candy. James was working a two-hundred-a-day habit but wasn't addicted, just used it to stay up. A grand was nice, four or five days of floating.

And there was the limo.

Except that Rissden had it wired with a silent alarm that went off in his briefcase and he and two of his employees—Turk and Jared—were on the way down in the elevator, just about to walk out into the parking lot when the alarm went off.

The first James knew what was happening was when he was leaning over to jam the key release and start the engine.

The door flew open and he was jerked out like a pup, hanging by his jacket.

"You want us to bust him some?" Turk (James learned their names later), who was the larger of the two men asked—although to James they both looked like giants.

Turk asked this of a man in a dapper linen suit. He was small but well-built, had salt-and-pepper gray hair, a neatly trimmed beard and thin lips that went straight across his face. To James he looked like he'd always had money, lots of money, all the money in the world. His named was Carlyle Rissden although James never heard him called anything but Mr. Rissden.

Initially Mr. Rissden had nodded and Turk hit James in the kidneys so hard he knew he would piss blood for a week. He did it silently and efficiently and was about to hit him again—James had stopped breathing—when Mr. Rissden held up his hand.

"Why were you stealing my car?"

James couldn't answer at first and struggled not to puke. He held it down, caught his breath. "I don't have anything and my wife and two kids are against the wall, mister, and if I don't get . . ."

Rissden nodded and Turk hit him again. The other kidney.

"Again. Why were you stealing my car?"

James threw up this time, down his shirt, and Rissden delicately stepped back and waited for an answer. James decided not to lie.

"For money. I was going to sell it to a chop shop."

Mr. Rissden nodded. "And this chop shop, do they buy many cars from you?"

He nodded. "Whatever I bring."

"What do they do with them?"

"Like the name says. They cut them up and sell them for parts . . ."

"How much would they make on a car like mine?"

"I don't know." He felt Turk tense again to hit him and he held up his hand. "No, I mean I really don't know. Maybe seven, eight grand. On some of them they change the serial numbers and paint the cars and resell them in another state. Then maybe they make fifteen, twenty grand. I don't know."

Mr. Rissden looked at Turk. "Don't you think it's interesting how fast he came around to our way of thinking?"

Turk said nothing.

"And he's pretty, too." Mr. Rissden smiled, touched James on the cheek. The touch felt cool, gentle, and yet powerful somehow. Gentle power—and completely, totally vicious. Without mercy if need be.

James shivered at the touch.

"Let's take him home, shall we?"

Still Turk said nothing.

"But first, a little business. I wish to take over this . . . this chop shop. It sounds lucrative. You gentlemen take care of it for me, will you? I, of course, don't want my name involved. Use the customary methods to handle the situation and take Mr. . . ." He looked at James. "I don't believe we got your name?"

James thought about lying, then decided they could take out his billfold and find it anyway. "James Vachon."

"Not Jimmy?"

"Nobody calls me Jimmy."

"Indeed. I guess you do look more like a James at that. Or would if you were dressed properly. Very well." He turned back to Turk. "Take Mr. James Vachon here with you so that he can understand how we operate and when you're done bring him home. I'll take a cab."

"Yes, Mr. Rissden." Turk nodded.

Rissden turned to go back into the elevator and then stopped, looked at Jared and Turk and James again, each in turn. "Isn't it wonderful how things happen? Just when I was starting to get bored Fate hands us this little trinket to play with—a chop shop. Indeed. Who would have thought it?"

He stepped into the elevator and was gone.

"Get in the back seat," Turk said. His voice was as strong somehow as his arms had been. James thought of running—they didn't know him, really, didn't have his address—but the voice stopped him. It wasn't rude, mean, not even threatening—just strong. Hard—like stone. Jared hadn't said a word yet but his manner, the way he moved his shoulders, made James think of a fighter—the men he'd seen in prison who worked the weights all the time and boxed in the gym. The men who could hit you and kill you with one blow if they wanted to . . .

He got in the car.

The problem was the chop shop. If he went with them and Harris—the guy who ran the shop—knew James had fingered him he was as good as dead anyway. Harris was not as strong as these men perhaps but he was mean, completely mean.

Maybe I can rabbit it on the way down, James thought as Turk backed the car out of the parking place and started out of the underground lot. Jared sat next to him, looking out the window at nothing, whistling some tune through his teeth.

They'll stop at a corner and I'll jump and run. James nodded to himself.

As if reading his mind Turk hit the lock master switch and James heard his door lock thunk into place.

He could still lie about the location of the shop, but that would only prolong things. Jared would probably start breaking his fingers or legs or something. He'd seen them do that to a man in prison. Some little asshole named Weally had stolen a porno magazine from one of the other cons and he'd picked the guy's favorite "paper wife."

It was like that inside. Either the men got together or they got magazines and married the girls in the magazines. There was a big business in porn in the joint. Men would pick their favorites and sleep with the magazine, hang blankets around their bunks to be alone with the magazines—just like they were alive. James had seen men fight over a picture of a woman and knew one con who had a whole business just renting magazines. So when Weally took the man's favorite magazine it was the same as taking the guy's wife and the man had gone crazy. He got Weally in the corner of his cell away from the television cameras, taped his mouth shut and broke every finger and both thumbs while James lay up in the top bunk and watched and heard the bones snap.

Like sticks.

So he couldn't really lie about where the shop was, either.

"Where we going?" Turk asked, looking in the mirror.

"What?" James asked.

"I said give me the address of the shop."

James nodded, hesitated.

"Now."

"Down on Hoyden. Between First and Second Street. There's a big red garage door and what you do is stop there and honk and they'll let us in."

"Not if they see *us,* they won't." It was Jared's first comment.

"How do we work it?" Turk asked.

"He drives," Jared said, pointing a thumb at James. "We hide in the back seat and he drives like he's stolen the limo and we get inside."

Turk smiled. "See? That's why we like you—you think of things. I told the boss just yesterday that I liked you because you think of things."

Two blocks from the shop Turk stopped the car and they exchanged seats. Both men scrunched down—James thought it was like trying to compress steel, watching them bend and try to get small—and they drove to the door of the shop.

It did not go like James thought it would go.

He had in mind that they would use muscle somehow and that there would be a fight and he could run then, run and get the hell out of town. He had a sister out in Oakland and he could go there and hide for awhile until things cooled down. Or maybe forever. He didn't know if any of these people—Rissden, Harris at the shop—any of them were connected but if they were he would have to change his name and find a whole new life because those sons of bitches never stopped looking.

But it didn't go that way at all.

He stopped the limo at the door to the garage, honked, the door opened and he drove in.

Inside there was chaos. The smell of torches and burning metal and rubber filled the air and it was hard to hear yourself think in the noise of grinders and hammers and pneumatic wrenches. Eight men with tools worked constantly, didn't look up as James drove the limo inside.

They could strip and dismember a car in thirty minutes, flat.

Harris was a thin man with a beer gut and a constant stink. James could smell it as soon as he got out of the car.

"You got a limo," Harris said, or started to say, then stopped as Turk and Jared got out.

"What's this shit?"

"I didn't have any choice . . ."

"Are they cops?"

"No." Turk cut in, smiling. "Although you'll probably wish we were." He nodded to Jared who stepped forward and put the barrel of a small pistol to Harris's head and pulled the trigger.

Pop.

It happened so fast that nobody had time to move, say anything—just pop and Harris dropped, dead when he hit the floor.

"Jesus." James stared at Harris's body. "You killed him."

There was, for the first time that James could remember, complete silence in the shop. Tools, hammering had stopped and everybody stared at the three men and Harris lying on the floor.

No blood, James thought—there was almost no blood. Just pop and a little hole and it was all over for Harris. It was all so . . . professional. Jared had probably done this many times before. Jesus. Like shooting a chicken or something. Like he didn't care.

"Who is the shop foreman?" Turk asked the watching men. They were all Mexicans and many of them could not speak English. All of them knew violence, knew death. That was part of their life. So was silence. It would be insane to admit anything to the man with the little gun. They said nothing.

"It is not to kill you." Turk waved a hand and the gun disappeared. He pointed to Harris's body. "This man angered some men about some other business and he had to be handled. We need somebody new to run the shop. If you think you can run this shop and want to be rich, step forward."

For another moment, two breaths, nobody moved. Then a man stepped forward.

"I am Salvo. I am the foreman."

"Can you run this business?"

"Better than that piece of shit ran it," he said, pointing to Harris's body. "He was forever with pussy and not watching us."

Turk nodded. "Then you will take his place. We will pay you what he was paid and I will give you one thousand dollars now for yourself and a two hundred and fifty dollar bonus for each of the other men to settle the business." He waved again to Jared who stepped forward and from the inside of his coat brought out an envelope with money in it.

He carries that all the time, James thought. He was still trying not to look at the body. An envelope full of money. Jesus.

Jared paid them, first Salvo, then each man.

"I will also give you another thousand to take care of this body," Turk said, and he nodded to Jared who handed the foreman another handful of money. All fifties, James saw—all crisp new fifties. He must carry a hundred grand on him. Jesus.

"I wish the body to be taken far from here and dropped with no way to identify it."

"Done." Salvo said, nodding.

"Here is my card," Turk said, handing a business card to Salvo. "Memorize my name and the phone number and if there is any trouble—*any* trouble—you are to call me and leave a message on the machine and I will get back to you. Do you understand?"

Salvo nodded.

"I will come each Friday to get money and go over the books, is that understood?"

Another nod.

"If there is something wrong with the books or I find that you have been cheating or holding back money we will do worse to you than to this man." Turk pointed to the body. "Do you understand?"

Salvo looked down at the body again and nodded slowly.

When they had driven in the garage door had closed behind them. Turk now nodded to a man who stood with his hand still on the button next to the door—his mouth open—and nodded. "You can open it now. We'll be going."

Jared and James climbed in back and Turk drove out and away, again in silence and all James could do was sit in the back next to Jared and think Jesus.

CHAPTER TEN

TALLY HATED HIS apartment.

It was, he thought, walking in the front of the building, that there was nothing there for him. Either he worked, and all his work was away from the apartment, or he was with Kari or wanted to be with Kari.

The apartment always seemed like it belonged to somebody else and he sometimes thought he kept it mostly just for a place to keep his phone answering machine.

He made it through the entry and the hallway without meeting anybody. The apartment building had seen better days, gone downhill and was now on the way back up as one of those "in" places to rent and remodel—a kind of unestablished condo—and there were always people from some improvement group or another waiting for him. But this time he was lucky and unlocked the door and stepped in without being bothered.

The smell was flat. Old clothes, no air movement, heat, an open beer on the counter in the kitchen—a single bachelor apartment smell.

He hosed the sink out and made a pot of coffee, turned on the classical station, opened a window and sat on the couch for a moment, drinking coffee and thinking.

He'd stayed with Kari two days and on the second day, while she was training, he'd sipped tea and sat at the table on the porch to look at the files Tyron had given him.

In his years he'd seen many horrible things. He was a grunt in Nam and had worked El Salvador and gone into Nicaragua with a contra group—journalism meant, really, seeing the worst. Blown-apart bodies, tragedy heaped on tragedy until it was almost impossible not to be toughened by it. The scars covered everything, even sensitivity.

And the pictures in the file—terrible as they'd been to Kari—were not nearly as bad as some things he'd seen and lived.

The children in the pictures—four boys and two girls—were all dead, were all nude and all beaten out of shape. None of them—except for the beatings and the damage done to the bodies—showed any signs of undue violence or mutilation.

They seemed to be almost peaceful and in some way that made them worse, more terrible. They were, somehow, almost *clinically* dead. What had been done to them was bad, was awful, was not to be believed, but the death was so cold, so heartless it made Tally think of the camps, the death camps, and the pictures and stories he'd read of them. Techni-death. Meant-death.

It was as if the children had been born, lived, done all the children things they were meant to do and all of it with the mark of death on them, all of it so they could end this way, in a police photograph with eyes glazed and dead.

He'd put them back in the envelope, the pictures, because he found he could not read the reports with them staring at him.

The reports were all dry, in police-ese, again without feeling—as they had to be. All the children had been sexually molested.

A given.

The thought came in that way as he was looking

at the reports. Just slipped in. Why was that? Why was it a given that children were sexually molested?

They were always the victims, somehow. In history the children suffered most. In wars and famine, in hate they died—in the Iran-Iraq war the bastards used them to clear mine fields by walking them through until they were blown up, told them they would go to Allah for it.

They were *always* the victims. But why was it so often, almost always sexual? Why was that a given? Why did everybody who was sick go after them that way?

Some . . . *thing,* some vulnerability, some gentleness drew them, drew the slime to them in homes and churches and day care centers, on streets and playgrounds, like wolves waiting to take sheep.

It was staggering, how often it happened. Once Tally had done a story on it, on children being victims and he'd spoken to a counselor who told him that it was probable that half of all children, a full *half* had been sexually molested at some point in their childhood. The counselor had been studying it for close to a decade, speaking to adults about what it had been like when they were young and he spoke of a car full of women going to a conference—six of them, all teachers. One of the teachers had a student she felt was being molested and brought it up and on the spur of the moment asked the women how many of *them* had been "bothered" (as she put it) when they were young.

All of them.

It could be more than half, the counselor said, perhaps as much as seventy-five percent of all children have to face it at one time or another. And they have no tools to deal with it.

A given.

All the children in the files had been killed by drug injection. The drug used was called T-60 solution, a veterinary drug used to put animals down, and it killed usually within ten to twenty seconds.

All of the children had been sodomized, all repeatedly, and none of it, none of it was anything Tally wanted to write about. None of it was anything he *would* write about because it did no good—people didn't do anything about it except react in horror and then go on with their lives. It was, sadly, a dead issue—except for the business with Tyron being taken off the case.

That didn't work.

That made everything different.

And there was the thing about the bodies—that drew him as well. They were all so consistent. All killed the same way, all nude, all beaten out of shape and all left in the country. It was so strange. Almost as if they'd been thrown away—like garbage. Was it something kinky, the way they were thrown away?

Enough. It was all right to have hunches, to work them, to get smells or hints and follow them, but outright guessing was wrong. Kid stuff.

Two of the bodies had been outside Tucson and he would have to go down there. That meant money. He'd sold a series of stories on slavery in America—it was possible to "buy" people, into a kind of indentured servancy, all legal and above board—to a national syndicate for seventeen thousand and there was still most of that left.

Plus he had paid up plastic so he could move and he put the files down and finished the tea and decided how to make it work. Just start digging—that had been his experience in other stories, in all stories. You poked and prodded and dug and things broke loose, people got scared and talked, a call would come in the night—something always happened.

So he'd left Kari—it was getting harder all the time—and drove to Denver and opened his stale door to his stale apartment and sat to drink coffee. He checked his mail, which he'd picked up on the way in, and it was all bills and bulk rate. He never opened bulk rate and threw it all aside for later.

And, finally, he pushed his answering machine button.

There were two calls from Kari—telling him to bring some things for salad when he came, which he'd missed—one call from Tyron, saying it wasn't important and that he'd try again and last, a voice he never expected to hear—a call from Andy Kleinst.

"I'm on to something you might find interesting," the voice said. "Give me a call."

And he left his number.

Tally leaned back in the couch and smiled. Andy Kleinst. What in hell did he want?

The last they had spoken was six, no five years ago in El Salvador. They'd both been down there as stringers except that Tally was being paid by a wire service and Andy was hacking for the tabloids, looking for what he called "juice."

Then some nuns had been in the wrong place at the wrong time and had been raped and murdered. Tally had gone to cover it and had found Andy there ahead of him. The nuns—four of them—had been laid out and their clothes straightened, each of them shot in the head and Andy hadn't liked the composition.

To Tally's utter disgust Kleinst had talked one of the guards into helping him rearrange the bodies into attitudes of violence so the pictures would be more sensational.

It had been done before, of course. In fact it was done often in combat photography. Seldom was death dramatic and good to photograph. It happened where it happened and that did not always mean the picture would be composed well. In the

Civil War Healy had bodies pulled all over the place for pictures, sometimes using the same body several times.

But journalism had changed. During the Civil War it was considered proper to use fiction to "enhance" truth. Exaggeration was considered proper form and taken into account by the reader. This gradually phased out—or should have—and something in Tally had snapped when he saw Andy working at the bodies, pulling them this way and that, the fat, little sweaty man. . . .

He'd walked over and hit Andy once, just in back of the ear, a professional punch that didn't move more than eight inches, a punch from his fighting days and Andy had gone down like a poled ox, had fallen directly on the dead nuns he was trying to arrange.

"What the hell. . . ." He'd mumbled, rolling over and getting up, rubbing his head. "What's the matter with you?"

"We don't do that," Tally had said.

"What's the difference? They're dead, aren't they? They don't give a shit."

"We don't do that," Tally repeated.

"I'm just trying to make a living here, get something I can sell. Who the hell are you to tell me what to do?"

"We don't do that." Strangely Tally wasn't even very angry. And as a point of fact there were many who still did it, many who "arranged" the news to make it sell. Especially for television. He'd seen network anchors ask people to do things over again to show how it had gone. What the hell *was* the difference? The nuns had been raped, tortured, killed—why couldn't Andy make it look more sensational?

But he knew he would hit Andy again and Andy knew it as well, could see it in Tally's eyes.

"All right. So shit, *we* don't do that. . . ." And Andy had taken what pictures he could and had walked away leaving Tally feeling sad—for the broken figures of the nuns on the ground—and slightly embarrassed at his own behavior.

And now there was a message from Andy.

Four, five years since he'd seen the man, since he'd dropped him.

How strange that the little shit would be calling him.

He put his coffee down and dialed Andy's number.

CHAPTER ELEVEN

Davey Hascombs was afraid.

There were many other feelings mixed in with the fear.

He was really and truly and honestly pissed off with himself for following the big geek with all the hair to his goddamn car.

That was *so* stupid. After all the things everybody said about geeks and assholes like this he'd gone and done it, just followed him to the car because he thought he was going to get some dumbshit old video game.

"Where are you taking me?"

"To the land, my boy, of milk and honey. To the promised land of milk and honey."

Davey's hand moved towards the seatbelt release and the big man reached over and slapped him, once, so hard across the side of his head that his ears rang. "I can hit you again if it's needed."

It was all so goddamn asshole shit *stupid,* Davey thought. To just go and follow him that way.

Some part of him had made him careful and he had held back, walked a little in back of the man as he went to the car. But there had been no threatening gestures, nothing said or done by the man to make Davey think he was in danger and when the man had opened the back door of the car and taken out the big box with the video game and controls Davey had thought it was all right.

Stupid.

The man had turned with the box in his hand, held it out for Davey to see and when Davey came close the man had reached out—like a snake striking—and his hand had closed on Davey's arm and Davey could not believe it.

"Get in the car without fighting," the man had said. "Or I'll kill you."

And Davey had been so scared—had hung in the

man's hand like a dead cat—so scared that he'd let the man take him around the car and into the front seat where the man locked the seatbelt around him tight, tight so he couldn't breathe, and they drove away and he couldn't believe how stupid he had been.

"This is wrong, you know. To take me like this. This is really, really wrong and they'll get you for it."

"Boy," the man turned and smiled at him, a large smile that wasn't really funny, "boy, they won't even come close. Ain't nobody going to get the Rev."

The man drove easily, controlling the big car with one finger on the wheel, not speeding, not seeming to be worried. He played country and western music on the radio, not loud, but enough so he could hear the words and sing along on some of the parts. Davey didn't know where they were—they were already out of his neighborhood—but he saw the ocean once or twice off to the right a ways and knew that meant they were heading south.

He saw police cars. Two of them right away, then another one in a little while and hoped that they would see him, hoped and hoped so hard that he thought they would be able to read his mind and feel his fear and would turn around and come back and catch this big asshole geek shit of a man and save him.

Save him.

On the third police car he couldn't stand it and he raised his hand and waved frantically at the cop but the cop didn't see him, was looking down, and the man hit him again, this time harder, much harder, and he slumped over against the door with his thinking all fuzzy for a few minutes.

Stupid.

After a little time—the clock on the dashboard of the car didn't work—the man turned off the freeway into an old neighborhood with big trees that almost covered the street. Davey watched as they drove down the street and saw that it was all houses and there were kids playing in the yards and he thought how lucky they were not to have been stupid enough to follow the man for some dumb old shit video game.

He could not believe that people didn't come to save him. They would look at him as the car passed, look right at him and he was so scared he was almost pissing his pants but they didn't see it. People didn't see it and they would look away.

Suddenly the man turned the car into a narrow, covered driveway that led to a garage. As they approached the garage the man pushed a button on a remote control and the door opened and they drove inside. The door closed and he turned to Davey.

"Here we are. Home again, home again, jiggety-jig."

"Where are we?"

But the man was already out of the car and had come around to Davey's side before Davey could react or even think.

He unhooked Davey's seatbelt and held his arm in the same iron grip, dragged him out of the car and to the door and into the house.

They walked through a kitchen—clean except for some dishes in the sink—down a hallway and into a small bedroom. There was a cot, made up with some kind of Indian blanket and no window. There had been one but it was covered with plywood screwed tightly in place.

Coming from under the bed was a chain about twice as long as Davey was tall and on the end of the chain was a handcuff.

The man put the handcuff around Davey's ankle and clamped it tight.

"Too tight?" he asked.

Davey nodded. "It hurts."

The man looked at his ankle. "It's not leaving any marks. That's the most important thing. No marks. The product can't have marks on it."

He didn't loosen the cuff but stood.

"The chain is bolted into the wall with an eyebolt. You can't get it out and I don't want you hurting yourself trying. If you're going to try and get away I can give you a shot to put you to sleep. It's a shot with a big needle. You don't want that, do you?"

Davey shook his head.

"Good. Then just stay cool and I'll bring you something to eat. You like pizza?"

Davey nodded. "I guess."

"And Coke?"

Another nod.

"I'll be back shortly. You rest and take it easy and don't hurt yourself, hear?"

And the man was gone.

Davey looked around the room again, pulled against the chain but it felt solid. He kneeled and looked under the bed and saw that it was locked into the wall with a heavy bolt. I couldn't break it with a hammer, he thought. Not with a big hammer.

He jerked a little more, then tried to get his foot loose and found there was some play there. It wasn't loose, but the big asshole shit hadn't made it as tight as he could and Davey found he could work the handcuff around part of his heel.

Just the top part.

A little at the top part but as he worked it the heel seemed to soften and it moved a little more. He took his shoe off and kept pushing at the handcuff, working it down against the meaty part of his heel.

If he could get loose and out of the room he would run and run and run.

The big asshole bastard shit would never catch him.

If he could get loose he would run and hide and never get caught and never, never even talk to strangers again even if they had video games.

If he could get loose.

CHAPTER TWELVE

BILLEE CARSTAIRS SET the phone down with practiced calm—Anne Bancroft in *The Graduate* couldn't have done it better—and felt in complete control of his world.

The call he had just received was from the born-again redneck peckerwood—or whatever they called them down there—telling him that they had another product.

"I have the product," the Rev had said—almost professional-sounding.

He had then gone on to whine and wheedle another five hundred out of Billee, which Billee had reluctantly—or seemingly reluctantly—allowed him to have. But in truth, Billee had always factored that into his expenses, knowing that somebody in what he called the "food chain" would soon get greedy.

The truth was, all expenses were still well within his plan. Everything was going according to plan.

They would have to party when this one was done, that's all there was to it.

He would have to throw a good party.

He would invite Jimmy and Barbara and the Caliph and that enormously rich Arab boy who had moved into the Hills—and had a different 'Cedes for each day of the week—and Wayne and Sessie and Peter.

Not a wild party.

An understated event, with no overtones—just let it go where it went and let everybody know, subtly and with finesse, let just *every*body know that he was successful in business.

They didn't have to know what kind of business, of course. That didn't matter. Business was business.

He moved product. He had employees and airplanes available to him and he moved product and that was all business was about. The product didn't matter. It was all profit and loss.

It didn't have to be something big, like nose candy or tootle. He was still good at it, and it was still business.

Business.

God, he felt good like this—successful and efficient. He would have to buy some new suits. Or maybe just a jacket. A new jacket to go with his new mood.

First he had to call Boston, the number in Boston, and arrange the transfer of product. First that. Business first.

Then he would make an appointment at The Boy's—they had the best suits. He would look for a loose-fitting gray, something subtle, and maybe a burgundy-and-gray ascot.

God, yes—perfect.

He picked up the phone and dialed the number in Boston.

CHAPTER THIRTEEN

ANDY PUSHED THE coaster aside with the bottom of his glass and used the wetness from the condensation to make little circles on the bar; around and around, little wet circles.

Tally waited.

He had called Andy and agreed to meet him at The Hoof—a bar on the edge of downtown Denver, a place mixed in a small shopping area with a bookstore, a tee shirt place, a video arcade.

Not . . . quite . . . a . . . dump. That's how Tally thought of it when he drove downtown and parked. The kind of place Andy would use.

Andy had been tight-lipped over the phone. Just said he wanted to meet Tally and talk something over. The call had been a surprise, that he wanted to talk to Tally was extraordinary and Tally had decided the best thing to do was follow it up and just let things come as they would.

"How have you been?" Andy asked.

Tally snorted. "Shit, get serious, Andy. You didn't call me down here to ask me how I've been."

"No." Andy sighed. "As a matter of fact I didn't. I called you down here to warn you."

"Warn me?"

Andy nodded. "You've got your dick in a pencil sharpener and there are some pretty big people holding on to the handle."

"Right." Tally laughed. "Let me get this straight—you're worried about me and want to warn me? Me? The man who knocked you on your ass?"

Andy smiled. "Yeah. I didn't think you'd buy it but what the hell—it was worth a shot."

"Translation," Tally said. "You're on a story and I'm cutting into it and you want me away from it—right?"

Andy stopped moving the glass, took a drink, put it down. Some kids came in. Tally knew they weren't over sixteen. The bartender served them without checking I.D.

"It's part of that," Andy nodded. "But there's a warning, too. I'm not shitting you on that, Janrus. You're walking into a faceful and don't even know it."

"I don't think you know what the hell you're talking about," Tally said. "I'm not 'working' on anything right now."

Andy sighed. "Look, if you're going to keep denying shit this won't get anyplace . . ."

Tally said nothing.

"You don't know what you're getting into," Andy said again. "This isn't jacking around with some shitheaded guerillas in the jungle. This is serious."

Murdered and raped nuns weren't serious, Tally thought. But still he waited, took a sip of his drink.

"You have to give me some credit. I've been in this business as long as you. I have contacts—have them all over the place. The truth is you're working on this kid thing and I know it. That's fine, or would be, except that I'm working on something too. *Not* the same story." Andy held up his hand. "Not even close. But I keep running into your name."

Tally couldn't believe that Mel Tyron had told anybody about giving him the files, or spoken about it. But Andy was scared—scared of something. The bar was cool—air-conditioned and the cool air kept moving by big ceiling fans—but Andy was sweating. His round face wet, his shirt damp.

He was told to warn me off.

That was it—the son of a bitch was sent to get me off the story.

But why?

What in hell was going on here? Who in hell would want to protect whoever is doing this to kids?

"Do you have anything for me?" Tally asked.

Andy stared at him.

"Come on."

"You're nuts," Andy said. "Just fucking nuts. Do I *have* anything for you? Christ, man, I'm trying to save you some grief here. You don't know these people."

"What people?"

Andy stared at him. "I don't believe you. You're talking to me like I'm some kind of hick, pushing the questions."

Tally smiled to himself. Andy was right. He was pushing the questions. It was an old technique—a gentle push, all the time, until something opened. But it worked. Even on other reporters.

"What people?"

Andy shook his head. "It doesn't matter. None of that matters. What counts is that you're jerking around on this kid thing and it's pissing people off. I hear things, overhear things and I thought I would warn you."

Right, Tally thought—you're saving my ass for me. Right. And the world rides on the back of a big turtle. He wondered if it would help to keep pushing, decided it wouldn't.

Tally stood. "I've got to go wash my shorts."

Andy looked up at him. His face was desperate. "Sit down."

Tally stood, thinking, then sat down slowly. Andy was scared. Tally had seen him be a lot of things—disgusting, stupid, even revolting. But not scared this way.

"I'm rummaging around, see," Andy said. "Digging in my contacts. Some of my best stories come from rummaging around."

"Kill fees," Tally said. "Some of your best kill fees."

Andy nodded unabashed. "That, too. You joke about it, but it gets the same job done. I catch some influential politician wagging his weenie and write about it, he quits. Or I can make him pay me to not write about it and hc quits. You get the same thing."

"No," Tally said. "You don't."

"Well, whatever. Just the same, I'm digging around in my contacts and I hear you're working on this kid thing."

"What contacts?"

"No." Andy shook his head. "You don't get that. Not even a hint."

"Was it a cop?"

"Stop it or I let you walk."

Tally closed his mouth.

"So I knew about the kid thing," Andy said. "But it's not what I do."

There's no money in it, Tally thought. Just dead kids.

"I mean nobody gives a shit about the kids anymore—or maybe never did, I don't know. But I know it doesn't make a good story. There's kids getting wasted all over the goddamn place. You can write a tearjerker and get some old lady crying about it but that's it. There's nothing there. No juice."

Why the hell am I sitting here listening to this shit, Tally thought. Journalism 101. He started to stand again.

"So I ran into your name. My contact tells me you're working on this thing, this kid thing, so I think, Hell, maybe there's something here I don't see, you know? If somebody like you is working on this there must be something here." He smiled. "Basic reasoning. So I dig a little more and all I find is kids that get buggered and killed. I mean it's no story, right?"

Jesus, Tally thought—*get* somewhere with this before I go to sleep.

"So I figure you're just doing some do-gooder shit and I drop it." The waiter came and Andy ordered another drink. Just one, for himself. Class, Tally thought—he always had class.

"Then I get a call."

Ahh, here it is—here's what I waited for, Tally thought. "What kind of call?"

"Just a call. But it's from somebody I know—and believe me, he's heavy. And he tells me to tell you to drop it."

Tally waited again, then sighed. "That's it? Drop it?"

Andy shook his head. "No. He said it wasn't something that could be changed and that it should be dropped."

"Nothing else?"

Andy paused, took a sip from the new drink. "Listen, I know you don't think much of me."

That, Tally thought, is one hell of an understatement.

"But we're the same, you and me."

"No. We're not."

"I know that's how you think, but we are. The same genes or something. This goddamn digging after the story—it gets us the same way. Well, as soon as this guy calls and tells me that I know it's something big, you know? I mean it stinks, smells to beat hell. And I decide to get into it. Maybe there is a story here after all, I decide.

"So I talk some more to a contact and then I walk out to the parking lot of this place—I mean not ten minutes had gone by—and there's this guy waiting. The kind with no neck. And he tells me I don't want to do what I'm doing and I believe him and I'm telling you."

I wonder how much they're paying him? Tally decided to ask. "How much are they paying you?"

"Paying me?"

"Yeah. To drop it, to get me to drop it. How much?"

Andy snorted. "You don't understand, do you? These people aren't like us—they don't even breathe the same air we do. They live in a completely different world. They have it all, Janrus—everything. Money, time and most of all, power. They can do anything they want, any time they want, and the laws, the rules don't apply to them. What I get is, I get my ass. And if you have any brains at all you'll do the same—settle for your ass."

Tally stood and left. There was nothing else to get from Andy and on the way out to his car he decided that none of what Andy had said was anywhere close to the truth.

Andy wouldn't do, or start to do any story that didn't have a buck in it. He only worked for money. Raw money. It wasn't getting the story published that counted to him. It was how much he could get paid not to publish.

And Andy was scared.

Really scared. It was in his eyes, the corners of

his eyes. A live fear. The kind of fear that came with combat—that pinch out at the corners that meant he was afraid.

Afraid to die.

So he was lying and he was afraid—so what? Tally started his car, pulled into traffic. What did it mean?

Things were never as they seemed—not ever. But in this case the lie was so pointed, so obvious that there had to be a secondary meaning.

He was told to warn me off, Tally thought.

And threatened. Told that if he didn't warn me off something would happen to him. There could be no other reason. Andy Kleinst didn't give a single pellet of rat shit about Tally—would just as soon see him dead, for all of that. He wouldn't cross the street to help Tally but the warning was valid. Somebody wanted him off this thing.

Somebody.

But who?

He let his brain chew on it while he drove—not thinking of driving.

The answer was back at the source. He would have to start over. Go back to Tyron and talk to him. He might be able to provide some names—or hints of names, or thoughts of names.

There was a time in any story when it wobbled. Some stories didn't get written even though they seemed valid. They would come to the wobble time and there wouldn't be enough to keep them alive.

This one had just passed the wobble point.

Andy had pushed it past. They—somebody—knew a whole hell of a lot about what Tally was doing. That in itself was interesting. But that they would get Andy to talk to him before he had even started, hadn't even begun to dig at the story. . . .

Definitely, Tally thought, driving—definitely past the wobble point.

He saw a pay phone you could use from the car and he pulled in to call Tyron.

CHAPTER FOURTEEN

AND SO JAMES had learned from Rissden.

It had come slowly at first because even after he'd seen what Rissden had done at the chop shop he didn't understand. Not all of it. Not the completeness of what Rissden was, how he operated.

He became the driver of Rissden's cars and found that driving the limousine or the Mercedes was like being a cashier at a bank—there was much more than he would have thought to the job.

The car was an extension of Rissden's office, his life. And James was part of that extension. Part of Rissden's life.

After the incident at the chop shop James had gone home to Rissden's with Turk and Jared and found that he was expected to nance with Rissden and that hadn't been so bad. Not as bad as prison—not nearly as bad as prison.

But Rissden didn't do it so much for the sex as for the control, the power. As a matter of fact he found later that Rissden preferred women and after that first time James wasn't expected to do anything but drive and help Jared and Turk "handle" things.

It was incredible—what Rissden was into—just unbelievable.

Anything and everything.

At first James had thought it was just somebody using muscle and if Turk and Jared weren't there nothing would have worked. Rissden might be the boss, but he had seen Turk and Jared work and they made the machine go.

But he was wrong. Turk and Jared were like James—just gears. Rissden was the engine, was the power.

He controlled everything he touched.

During the first three months James worked for him—and he was paid a grand a week, in cash, in an envelope each Friday—he had watched in constant amazement.

"The idea," Rissden had said once, sitting in the back with Jared while James drove and Turk sat next to him in the front, "is to make money."

And he meant it.

Gambling, some drugs, extortion, loan sharking, hookers—Rissden was in all of them. He owned apartment buildings, condos, a shoe store. In a given day he might be talking to a pimp who ran a stable for him and a shoe wholesaler and when Rissden talked it was like the broker:

Everybody listened.

In the case of the pimp he found that the man had been keeping too much money and he had quietly told Turk to break his arms.

"Snap something," Rissden had said from the back of the limo. "His arms. Snap something so he understands."

Turk and Jared had put the pimp's arms on the curb and jumped on them and James heard the bones break even over the screams.

And with the shoe wholesaler it was the same. He had been charging a fair amount for the shoes sold in Rissden's shoe store—which was too much.

"There has to be pain," Rissden said to James in a conversational tone while Turk and Jared were turning the wholesaler's face into strawberry jam. "Without pain there is no knowledge of truth. . . ."

Everywhere and anywhere he saw opportunity. Rissden moved as he had with the chop shop.

"Being flexible," he said, "is the key to success."

Once they were driving towards an apartment building where Rissden allowed a select, small game to work in one of the upstairs apartments. Only high rollers were allowed in—one hundred thousand minimum buy-in—and Rissden furnished the dealer, food, drinks, women and the place for a ten percent rake from each pot.

They were driving to get his skim when James pulled out to pass a semi full of coffins.

Coffins.

The name of the company was on the side of the truck, along with their address, and Rissden had suddenly leaned forward in the seat.

"James." He tapped him on the shoulder, smiling. He liked to say the name—James. Once around the park and home, James. "See the address on the coffin truck? Take me there after we check on the game."

So they had gone to the coffin factory.

It hadn't been much of a factory. Just a large metal building where they made wooden coffins but Rissden had walked in and spoken to the owner and come back out in ten minutes.

"Coffins." He'd said. "Perfect, don't you see? There are no codes, no rules—just as long as the bottom doesn't drop out at the wrong time. They can be made out of the cheapest materials and you can charge the highest prices—take advantage of the grief. It's perfect. See to it, will you Turk?"

So James and Jared and Turk had driven back later and Turk had gone inside and in a little time had come out with a thin man in a suit. He had large eyes and nervous hands and was so afraid that Turk hadn't even had to hit him. Turk just put him in the back of the limo and sat with him and explained everything slowly, how Mr. Rissden wanted to own a share in a place that made coffins.

And Rissden owned a coffin factory.

Wherever there was money, James thought in genuine admiration, was where Rissden would go. And he always won. Always.

It was not until he'd been driving for Rissden for over six months that he found out about Rissden's catering service—or at least a kind of catering service.

"We cater to parties," Rissden said once and Turk had smiled. "Special parties."

Even then James did not understand. He thought Rissden meant drugs, or perhaps hookers. Which was true enough. James had gone with Turk to arrange for hookers to be brought to hotels or condos for "special" parties. These were not one timers or even all nighters but groups of hookers—sometimes eight or ten—for celebration purposes.

On one night James had driven a van with seven hookers in it while Turk had followed in the limo.

They'd taken the women—who were never silent, sitting in the back of the van telling stories of tricks they had turned—to a private home in a suburb and picked them up at nine the next morning.

James had no knowledge of the guests, or the reasons, but knew that Rissden moved in large, high circles and that, too, he'd found out by accident.

He'd taken Rissden to the airport one night about ten o'clock and as they pulled in Rissden had directed him around to a private gate where a guard was posted and let them through.

James was ordered to drive the limo out to a small Lear jet and four men emerged wearing suits that cost well over a grand each and carrying brief-cases. They were all middle-aged, all foreign—he could not tell where they were from (he knew nothing of accents) and they all treated Rissden like a servant.

That's what got James. Rissden was a hard man, a man with hard edges even when he played and these four men all but ignored him.

On the other side of the coin Rissden went out of his way to be nice to them. He shook hands with each one, helped them into the car—there was some shuffling to get them all into the back seat of the limo comfortably—and then rode up front with James. Jared and Turk—never away from Rissden—followed in another vehicle.

The four men had not spoken to Rissden but

had talked among themselves. They spoke in English but with an accent and they talked of small things. Presents for wives, new cars, a boat one of them was buying—James realized after a moment that the "boat" was an ocean-going yacht when the man said it took a crew of thirty to man it correctly.

"We must do this on the boat sometime," he had said. "We'll let the crew have liberty and we'll relax. The sea air should be most invigorating."

James had half-listened to them. He was unused to Rissden riding in the front with him and he'd worked hard to drive correctly. It was strange but of all the feelings he held for Rissden—fear, respect, confusion—the one most prevalent was awe.

He had such complete control of his life, everything around him, was so goddamn powerful that James thought of him as more than human in some way.

And these men treated Rissden like a servant.

And he had accepted it.

Once later he'd asked Turk about it but Turk had ignored him—which he did in most cases anyway. James never asked Jared about anything. Jared didn't seem to want to have anything to do with James and that was fine with him. Jared had cold eyes and even when he smiled it was straight across and dead.

Rissden had told James directions to take the four men one turn at a time and twice he knew he'd gone around blocks so that Rissden could check on a tail. He supposed it was some business, some close business—drugs, dirty money, he didn't know.

When they had come to a small house set well back into some old elms—almost completely hidden—with a long driveway Rissden had ordered James to turn in and he had done so, opening the doors for the men and Rissden.

"Wait with the car with the lights out," Rissden had said. "I'll be out in a few minutes."

So James had waited and while he was waiting another car had come up in back of him, the lights blinding him and a woman had gotten out of the car and walked past with another smaller, younger woman walking with her.

The lights had ruined his vision but he saw the two of them walk up to the door of the house and go in without knocking.

A few moments had passed and Rissden came out, walked to the limo and got in back. "Let's go."

Except that James had not been able to leave because the second car was blocking him.

"Move it. It's mine."

James had gotten out and found the keys were in the car and moved it out of the way so they could leave.

He lived in back of Rissden's house in an apartment next to the garage and at seven the next morning, while he was drinking coffee, the phone from the house had rung.

"Have the car ready in fifteen minutes," Turk had said.

"All right."

In precisely fifteen minutes Rissden had come out and ordered James to drive. Again they had changed directions several times and again they wound up at the small house in the elms. Even in the daylight it was hard to see the house. The trees covered it completely, kept it partially darkened.

The car James had moved was still there, off to the side but partially in the drive as James had left it. He stopped rather than ease by it but Rissden ordered him to the house.

"To the door—right next to it."

He moved the limo forward, stopped, and the moment he had halted the door opened and the four men came out.

Dressed the same except that now they all had dark glasses on. Rissden moved up front and James held the door while they all got in back again.

"To the airport," Rissden said. "That same side gate."

James drove without thinking, half-listening to the men in the back. They spoke again of presents for their families, boats, planes. As they reached the airport one of them leaned forward and handed Rissden a business envelope.

Rissden put the envelope in the inside pocket of his coat. "Was everything to your satisfaction?"

"Indeed. Very much so—better than we had heard it would be. It was most . . . refreshing."

"Good."

"In fact we were discussing it this morning and wondered if it might be possible to do it again?"

"Of course." Rissden nodded, turning in the front seat to face the back. "In a different location, naturally. For security reasons."

"Ahh, yes, we understand security."

James took them to the same side gate, was waved through by a guard and thought what juice, what goddamn incredible juice these guys must have. To order Rissden around, then skip airport security and customs—assuming they were going to fly out of the country.

He drove them to the side of the Lear and opened the door to let them out and one of them handed him a bill which he stuck in his pocket, nodding his thanks and later he'd taken the note out and seen that it was a hundred dollar bill.

The man had handed it to him as if it had been a dollar. And he guessed that it had about as much weight to him.

God knows what they had paid Rissden. Thousands, probably—for one night with two women.

Or one woman.

And a girl.

He had seen her in the lights briefly as the two of them walked to the front door of the house and she had long, blonde hair. She had been walking stiffly, as if afraid—but James could have been wrong.

At least that first time.

He hadn't known then what was happening. Not exactly. The girl had been young but he had seen younger on the streets and he had heard cons talk all the time about men who had short eyes—men who liked boys and girls. It wasn't that odd. And they said that the kids liked it. Maybe not at first, but after a time—that's what they said.

So even at that James didn't think too much of it.

Not then—it didn't worry him at all then. And when it did bother him, when he found out what was happening and it bothered him it was only for a few minutes.

Life was a bitch, and it was hard all the time. You had to roll with it.

CHAPTER FIFTEEN

It was working.

Davey jerked and pushed at the handcuff until it was almost completely over the soft part of his heel. It kept sticking and finally he thought of spitting on his heel and that did it. The cuff slipped over the heel and down the foot and he was free.

Or sort of free.

He was in a small bedroom with plywood over

the windows and when he tried the door he found it to be locked.

He moved to the window and looked at the plywood but it was thick and screwed tightly into place with wood screws every few inches.

And so he wasn't free.

He cried for a time then, for the first time since the man had taken him. It would not help and he knew it but he couldn't help it and the tears came.

I am a goddamn dummy, he thought, crying. Just a goddamn dummy. I wonder what mom and dad are doing now. Probably drinking. They liked martinis and since dad closed that deal or did whatever it was he did—Davey didn't understand real estate—they would probably be drunk for a week.

The maid would miss him.

Maria would miss him. But not until really late. He usually didn't get in until evening anyway and she would just save him some dinner on a plate to nuke later and think he was off boarding or gaming. Probably she wouldn't think much until nine. Then she would tell Davey's mother and if she was sober enough they would call around but it would be ten or eleven or maybe even midnight if they were really drunk before they would call the cops.

And what good would that do?

They'd met cops and it didn't help and where would the cops look? They wouldn't know anything.

Davey didn't know anything and he was the one who was taken.

Taken.

What would they do to him?

He knew some of it. He had heard stories from other kids about the bums who lived in the bushes in the park. They were always trying to get kids to come into the bushes or the public bathroom that was so grody your feet stuck to the floor. This guy didn't look like a bum but maybe that didn't make any difference. He'd had a friend named Ben who said his uncle had tried to get funny with him and Ben had said his uncle was just as normal as anything until one day he put his hand on Ben's crotch and smiled.

Maybe this guy was that way. Or maybe it was a kidnapping for ransom. His folks had some money and maybe that was it.

He went to the door again, tried it. He thought he'd heard the car drive away when the man left and that he was left alone. When the knob didn't turn he threw himself at the door like they did in the movies and tried to kick it like the cops did but all he got was sore feet. The door was solid and locked tightly.

He sat on the bed again.

He needed a plan. It wasn't enough to sit and cry. He had to get out of here.

The man would come back soon and then what? Maybe the man was lying about pizza. Maybe he was coming back to do what the bums in the bushes at the park did.

He had to have a plan but his brain didn't seem to work. He was just scared, scared silly and couldn't think of anything to do.

So he sat on the bed for awhile and stared at the door and wished he had a big gun or a bomb or a laser gun and he could just kill anybody who came through the door.

In what seemed like a very long time he heard a car door slam and then a door in the house slam as well and knew the big man was home.

And he had a plan.

It came that suddenly.

He had to move fast to make it work. What he would do was wait by the door until the man unlocked it. Just then he would jerk the door in and run through and under the man and outside. Davey remembered the house. They'd come in the door from the garage, through a kitchen, but they had walked past a living room and there was a front door there. He'd seen it. He couldn't get out through the garage because the man would probably have closed the door.

But if he could get past the man and get to the front door and get outside there was no way they could catch him. He would run and run and they would never catch him.

He heard footsteps in the hall and he moved from the bed to the door. Crouched.

The footsteps moved past, heavy, then turned and came back.

Davey heard clicking as a lock was removed from a hasp on the door and he braced his legs.

The door started to open.

He grabbed the knob, jerked at it and hauled the door open and scrabbled through, keeping low and trying to move as fast as possible.

"What the hell?"

The big man was caught off guard and was thrown back against the wall of the hallway, momentarily off balance.

But he was not alone.

In back of him was a woman. She was heavy but not quite fat and had a smell like a hospital—that's all Davey knew before he ran into her. By then he was moving so fast his momentum knocked her down and he ran over her and was loose.

"Grab him! Grab the little shit!"

"Hell, *you* grab him!"

Was loose and moving.

He was down the hallway in less than a second and across the living room and at the door but it was locked. He jerked at the lock, got it loose, then looked up to see a chain lock holding it.

He heard footsteps in back of him, coming fast.

No time now, no time for the door. He left it

and crossed the living room in two leaps, over the back of a stuffed chair and through an opening to the door that led to the garage.

This was open and he plunged through into darkness. There were no lights and he tripped over a can and went down but bounded up and ran to the door. Next to the main garage door, which he knew opened electrically, there was a regular door. He could see the outline in the light from the door opening into the house and he grabbed at it, jerked, felt it move, then saw that it was padlocked from the inside and it stopped against the hasp.

Around the car.

They were nearly on him. Both of them were in the garage now and he ran around to the opposite side of the car. He stopped, heaving breath, watching them as they moved—one each way, the man and the woman, around the car. He had to lose them long enough to get back into the living room and get the chain lock off the door.

He'd seen daylight there—actually seen it. Was so close, so close. . . .

"You can't get away, boy." The man said. "There's no way you can get away from us."

Davey said nothing, watching them. The woman was the best chance for him. She was maybe not as strong as the man.

If he let them get close, then ran past the

woman maybe he could beat them to the door and get the chain loose.

Close now. Much closer. They moved in on him.

"Just take it easy, boy. We brought you pizza and Coke. You'll like it. I got extra cheese."

Now.

He ran into the woman again, felt her grab at his tee shirt, heard the material tear and was gone, his tee shirt ripped down the back.

Back into the house.

"Goddammit—grab his little ass." The woman this time, her voice low, tough-sounding.

The man jumped to cut him off and missed and Davey was inside the house, across the living room, had the chain, had the wonderful chain in his hand and it was loose and the door swung open and he was a step outside, a step gone when he felt the hand grip his arm.

"Not this time, boy."

The grip was hard, so hard it hurt and Davey was dragged back in the house. He pulled, struggled but it was no use.

"You act like you don't want to be here," the man said. "What's the matter with you?"

"Hold him." The woman came up. She was working to catch her breath and she took a small case out of the pocket of her jacket. "Let me give him a shot."

She opened the case and Davey saw that it contained a hypodermic. The man held him still and she expertly injected him in the upper arm.

"It'll take a minute or so," she said. "Then he'll be easy to handle."

"I hate doing this," the man said, "ever since we lost that one. It's such a risk."

"That was a freak accident. She reacted to the drug. Sometimes it happens—even in the hospital sometimes it happens."

Davey shook his head. Everything was getting brighter, louder, more funny. He laughed.

"See?" She put the needle back in the case. "It works fast. Now he'll be easier to handle, break in. It's better all around."

"I still like doing it the other way." Davey looked up at the man. His face was impossibly long, his eyes drooping. Davey laughed again.

"It's better with drugs," she said. "They're more relaxed."

"I still say it's risky. . . ."

"Mom." Davey looked up at the woman. Her face had changed to his mother's face. "Hi, mom." He wanted to ask her how she found him, tell her it was good to see her but the words wouldn't come. His mouth made a sound. "Nnnnnngggggh."

"Look at him." The man said. "He's in la-la land."

"Which is exactly where we want him for breaking in. He'll be all relaxed and easy to deal with. When they're stiff and scared it makes it harder."

"But he won't remember any of it."

"He'll remember—believe me." She took Davey's arm and he followed her readily. She was, after all, his mother. "Now come on—I'm only on a long break. I have to get back to the hospital or they'll dock my pay."

She led Davey back to the bedroom.

CHAPTER SIXTEEN

THE PILOT'S NAME was Aaron Feeds.

He never looked in the back of the pilot's seat—never looked at what he hauled, never cared, and probably because of that he had managed to hold on to his twin Bonanza, have a good apartment, put a little in the bank besides.

Oh, he'd had all the dreams that came with flying. First he was going to be a fighter pilot, a top gun, but he couldn't handle the academic standards. He soloed when he was seventeen, had his commercial license at nineteen and thought he'd have it made in the Air Force but they told him college and that had killed that.

So he decided to be an airline pilot. He worked at his multi-engine ticket and made it and had run into the same problem—they wanted college. Airlines were getting picky.

Then it was small airports and little jobs teaching flying, taking doctors on trips in charters, dragging drunks to football games, a year-and-a-half flying the bush in Alaska and booze.

Always more and more booze.

And that had finally done him in. He'd dumped an employer's Piper stopping for fuel on a ferry trip. It was in Iowa, at a small field in broad daylight with no wind and he just brought her down too hard, slammed her down so that the undercarriage gave out and the prop hit the cement and the shit hit the fan. He had a bottle in the plane and a lot of it in his gut and that had been the end of his regular employment.

Then somebody had come to him and asked him to fly from a small strip in Mexico to another small strip in Minnesota.

"What are we hauling?" he'd asked.

"Does it matter?" The man speaking to him was tall and had almost no neck and one hell of a lot of money in his coat pocket. He gave Aaron a thousand in used hundreds. "And four more when you get back."

Five thousand dollars.

And Aaron found that indeed it *didn't* matter what he hauled.

He made that run with no problems in a rented Cessna 210. Landed in Mexico with a prearranged signal where a Jeep came alongside the plane and put a package in the back seat. Aaron didn't turn around, didn't look, didn't speak, never cut the engine or even decrease speed and took off within one minute of landing.

He flew low then, stayed well below radar, well below most of the terrain and worked up across Texas, refueling twice at small town strips and timed it to arrive at the strip in northern Minnesota after midnight as instructed. There he landed, somebody in a pickup took the package—again without Aaron looking—and he took off, once more without cutting the engine or spending more than a minute on the ground.

When he got back to Tucson the man came to him and gave him the four thousand, plus an extra thousand for good service.

"I like the way you do business," Aaron had told him.

"There'll be more. Much more work. I want you to buy a plane, a good one—I'll front the money.

Call this number when you've found one you like and leave a message on the machine and I'll call you." He'd handed Aaron a card with no name, just a telephone number on it—with the area code of 617. Aaron had been curious enough to check on it and found it to be Boston but that's as far as he examined it, or anything else.

The money was good, was real, and he'd starved long enough. He didn't give a shit what they did. They were going to buy him a plane and make him rich and that was good enough.

He found the Twin Bonanza in Florida. It had just had a major overhaul and from the photos in the national plane market magazine looked to be in good shape. They were asking seventy grand, which was cheap—it was probably a repossession as most of them were—and called the number in Boston.

It took four days to get an answer and then the same man told him.

"I'll send the money. Buy it."

"I could probably get them down on it," Aaron had told him.

"Buy it."

Two days later, by express mail, he received an envelope with seventy thousand in it in used hundreds. He took a commercial flight to Florida, talked them down to fifty-eight grand, cash—it had been a repossession and the bank was glad to get the fifty-eight—and he pocketed the extra twelve.

The plane had been loaded. All the latest nav gear and state of the art computers and communications equipment and all he did was get a cushion to bring his ass up a bit and fill the tanks and fly home.

She was sweet, a dream to fly, and if there had been any doubts about what he was getting into they vanished on that flight back from Florida to Tucson. He'd worked in a zig-zag across the country, learning the plane and by the time he was in Tucson he was in love.

He had been doing most of his flying out of a small strip west of town and when he returned there was a message on his machine to call the Boston number.

"Move," the man told him.

"Where?"

"Somewhere they don't know you very well."

"It costs money to move," Aaron had said, thinking what the hell, it was worth a shot.

"You have the twelve left over from the money to buy the plane."

"How did you know that?"

The man ignored the question. "Just move. Within a week. And don't tell anybody where you are. Not anybody."

None of it was very difficult. He had no ties. One broken marriage years before, no children, and a long line of one night stands or at most a week, bar pickups. No family.

And they knew all of that, he thought, getting ready to move. The man with no neck knew all of that before he came to talk to Aaron. He was exactly what they wanted.

And they were exactly what he needed.

He was kept on a retainer of two grand a month and paid extra for each time he flew, which worked out to vary but averaged several times a month.

"All that's required of you," the man told Aaron over the phone—Aaron had never seen him again, "is that you keep the plane ready to go at any time and make no other commitments of any kind."

Aaron moved to Santa Fe, found a small apartment and set up a form of housekeeping. A machine for the phone and a place to sleep and the rest of the time drinking the afternoons away in slow comfort in a bar on the plaza or playing poker with a group of men in the back of the bar.

Twice a day he checked the machine for messages and when they came he stopped drinking immediately and answered them.

The jobs had been steady and yet all different.

Several more times he went to Mexico, once to South America, once to Colombia—which had been the worst. He always went alone, always worked alone, and the time in Colombia he had landed amidst a group of self-styled soldiers who thought they wanted not just the money the man in Boston had sent them but the plane, and Aaron's ass as well.

It had been tight then but he had the package in the back of the Bonanza and took off before anything actually developed.

The rest of them had been milk runs. For the past six months he'd been doing people, carrying people, but the checks came each month with the bonus for when he worked and he didn't care.

Not really.

Some of the people had been small people—he did not think of them as children somehow but small people, and some of those had been carried on wrapped in blankets—but the checks came each month and he didn't look in back.

The pay was the same, whether it was packages from Colombia or small people or men. They always got in back and sat quietly and didn't ask questions or make sounds and that was fine, would still be fine, but lately. . . .

Starting five months ago, no, four months ago they had taken to getting rid of things while he was flying. There was a hatch in back of the seats and they would order him to fly over open country and they would put something out of the hatch and when they landed there would be less getting off the plane than got on the plane.

If he thought of it, if he sat and thought at all of it he would know what they were doing but that was not how he was, not how he acted.

He drank instead. Professionally, in the bars on

the plaza, drank whenever he wasn't flying and the checks kept coming and he put them in the bank and for the first time in his life he had money in the bank, a plane free and clear and all the time he needed to drink.

What they did or did not put out the hatch in the back of the seats did not make any difference—not really. There was nothing he could do about it anyway. They knew him, the people who sent the money knew him, knew all about him and if he said anything about anything the man with the thick neck would come from Boston and Aaron would probably be the next package they put out the small hatch in back of the seats.

So he never looked in back. He enjoyed the plane and the money and the drinking and he never, never looked in back.

CHAPTER SEVENTEEN

TALLY PUSHED THE pad of legal paper away and took another cup of coffee.

He was back in his apartment and was trying to formulate some reasoning behind what was happening with the investigation.

It didn't make sense to him.

He had written a list of ideas, trying to tie them together.

Crazy A.H. (for asshole)
kids and dumps
them in country.

All over southwest?

Powerful people try to stop
investigation.

Why?

Politics?

Money?

He pulled the list forward again, looking for reason. It just didn't make sense. If the people running around doing kids were connected politically who would be stupid enough to protect them?

Why protect them? That had to backfire. The only time he could think of it paying off was with Jack the Ripper. He'd once done an article on the English killer and had agreed that the man doing it was probably royalty, or related to royalty, and had been protected.

But not this time—it just didn't seem to scan.

Look at it again. He drank coffee. Look at it one more time.

Bodies of children are found nude, battered almost beyond recognition in open areas of country, sexually molested by more than one person. Maybe more than two or three persons.

With no evidence except the semen and bite marks.

And that was it.

Then Tyron was taken off the case and now somebody had used Andy Kleinst to try take him off the case as well and none of it scanned.

He'd have to chip away at it.

He dialed the station and asked for Tyron, waited on hold for what seemed like hours and finally got through.

"Yeah." Tyron sounded frazzled.

"I hate to bother you but I'd like to see you again, talk to you."

"It wouldn't be good."

"I understand, but the pieces aren't coming together for me and you called and left a message for me to call you."

"There's one more thing," Tyron said.

"What?"

"Each body was found in an indentation in the earth."

"You mean buried? I didn't see that with the body I saw."

"Not buried—dented. The ground was dented."

"You mean beaten down?"

"Yeah."

"That's crazy."

"Just like everything else about this case. . . ." Tyron grunted.

"I need more," Tally said. "Tell me more about who told you what."

"No. There isn't anything more."

"Come on."

"No."

And he hung up.

Tally turned the switch off on the wireless phone and laid it on the table.

Dented.

Jesus, the kids were beaten down so hard they were *pounded* into the earth?

That was ridiculous. Some force, some giant force had smashed them so hard into the ground that they dented the dirt.

Could a man, even a large man be that powerful?

Myths came to Tally—the myths of combat and power. They were always wrong. That a man could be knocked down by a bullet was wrong—power didn't work that way. No bullet knocked down, not even the big ones. They went through. Too fast to knock down. It took a blast, a mighty shove to knock a man over.

To dent the earth.

No human power could do that. The tissue in

the children's body would give before it dented the earth.

So either the indentations were dug and somehow made to look compressed or. . . .

Or what?

Or the kids were slammed into the ground in some way, with such force as to make them compress the earth.

Dropped.

It came to him with a picture.

It had been a large, old fashioned maneuver of airborne troops. He'd been asked to cover it for some eastern paper—he couldn't remember the name of the paper—and he'd flown down to Alabama.

The airborne almost never used parachutes any more, having gone over to vertical assault with helicopters, but this was going to be a regular drop and indeed that was why the newspaper wanted it covered.

The story of a regular drop was getting more and more rare.

So Tally had gone and sat in some bleachers near a field to watch along with a bunch of dependents and congressmen there on a junket. Because he'd done these things before he'd brought binoculars and because he brought binoculars he saw everything closer than he would have seen it, closer than he wanted to see it.

The planes had come and everybody had looked up and the chutes started to blossom as the men—and a few women—began to drop. A photographer had come from the paper to shoot pictures and he was busy with a telephoto lens, snapping and whirring and Tally heard him say, "Shit."

Tally had looked where he pointed and saw that one man's chute hadn't opened, had streamered. It had been a high drop—three thousand feet—not a low combat drop where the chutes barely had time to open and the man had plenty of time.

Tally watched through the binoculars.

The man rolled on his back and ripped his reserve chute out like he'd been told to do, feeding it out from the belly pack with his hands and it deployed up and up and looked good, started to swell.

Then it tangled with the whipping main chute and the man was dead. All his options were gone and he knew it but he didn't give up. Tally watched, couldn't take the binoculars off him, all the way down and the man kept pulling and pushing at the shrouds on the reserve, trying to pop it open and was still working at it when he hit the ground.

Because he had been pulling two flapping, unopened chutes he had not achieved anything like terminal velocity. But he was going fast enough.

He hit with tremendous energy, seemed to drive into the earth. Dust whumped up all around. And he bounced. The body—he must have been killed instantly—bounced, or seemed to bounce a foot or so in the air and then settled back into the earth.

Settled, Tally thought, remembered the picture —settled into the earth.

The man had hit not two hundred yards from the bleachers and the photographer had jumped down to the front and run to get a closer shot of the body—he was, after all, a news photographer. But Tally had held back. He'd seen enough death, even then, and the binoculars had brought him closer than he wanted to be.

Close enough to see that the body had dented the earth.

He picked up the phone to call Tyron, was going to tell him, then decided against it. They had probably spoken too much over the phone already. There was a standing joke that stated if you couldn't tap the phones in a police station where *could* you tap them? All cops assumed their phones were tapped.

Plus Tyron seemed not to want to see him. So he tried a new tack and instead rang through and when the cop answered Tally merely said: "I'll buy the beer."

"Where?"

"The Pub."

"When?"

"Twenty minutes."

"Right."

And Tally had turned the phone off and laid it back on the charger base.

It took him fifteen minutes to drive to The Pub. It was a bar in conjunction with a steak house, one of those places that usually cater to up-style assholes—as Tally thought of yuppies—with more money than brains.

But somehow a mistake had been made and the place had hired a manager who knew what the hell he was doing. The cook was a no-nonsense chef from New Orleans who made everything he cooked memorable and the bartender knew when to keep his mouth shut and bring drinks. The place had been discovered by one of the stringers on the *Denver Post* and had become a hangout for reporters and bachelor men and women who hated to cook.

Tally was there in fifteen minutes and saw Tyron pull up as he got out of the car.

Tyron came over, smoking the inevitable cigarette. "What have you got?"

"The bodies were dumped from a plane."

"What?"

"Think on it. I remembered a drop I saw at Huntsville years ago. A trooper dented when he hit. How else would there be enough force to mess them up the way they are—to hammer them into the ground like that?"

"Planes." Tyron shook his head. "You mean the bastards have an air force?"

"Which puts us exactly where we were," Tally said, "nowhere."

Tyron nodded.

"How are the gang killings going?"

"Shit."

"Can you do anything on this?"

"What do you mean?"

They'd been walking towards the entry and Tally paused at the door. "I mean unofficially. I was thinking you could check with Tucson or Phoenix. Maybe somebody saw a plane, got some numbers or something."

Tyron shook his head. "Not in the open. I can work around it and get a little done. I'll try."

Tally held the door open. "I'll still buy you some pepper steak."

"That's what graft is all about, my boy," Tyron said, moving into the cool darkness of the bar.

Tally returned to his apartment close to six o'clock, turned on the answering machine and got Andy again.

"I need to talk to you. Again. I have something for you. Meet me . . . no, shit, never mind. I'll come to your place. I'll be there about seven. This concerns what we talked about and is very important."

Tally made coffee. The pepper steak had been

delicious and he and Tyron had spent the meal in small talk.

He drank the coffee.

He waited.

Seven came, then seven-thirty, then eight and he drank some more coffee.

And waited.

Andy never showed.

CHAPTER EIGHTEEN

DAVEY WAS SO happy.

The woman's shot had made him smile and she was so sweet with him and so gentle and smelled so nice that even when he figured out it wasn't his mother he didn't care.

Her hands were soft as they put him on a big bed in a different bedroom from the one he'd been in. She undressed him.

"He's cute, isn't he?"

The man said nothing more and was doing something in back of Davey by the door but Davey couldn't see it. The woman helped him lie down on the bed and took his clothes off and rolled him over on his stomach and talked to him and rubbed his temples the way his mother would sometimes do when he was sick and Davey was thinking, smiling and thinking, that all of this wasn't so bad.

Then the man did something that caused him pain, lots of pain.

He couldn't believe what the man was doing and he tried to get away, tried to turn and yell but it didn't work, nothing worked. The drugs made him numb and the woman kept talking to him, rubbing his temples and saying low things to him, telling him to relax, just relax, take it easy and relax but he couldn't.

Even when it was done that time and they left him alone for a little while while the woman went away and came back or later when the man did other things he couldn't believe, for the next two days or two weeks or two years, even with all the soft talk from the woman and more shots of the drugs he couldn't relax, could never relax again.

His body was rigid and he went into a kind of dream like the time when they had to operate on his tooth to straighten it so that it was all happening to somebody else.

Not somebody he knew, not a person with a name, but just another body. Another body.

It wasn't him—wasn't Davey Hascombs all this was happening to; wasn't Davey Hascombs crying and screaming; wasn't Davey Hascombs being held and hurt by the man and woman but some other person without a name.

With no name.

He lay or sat stiffly, however they put him, whatever they did to him and let his mind wander to see things that were in other places. He saw himself working with the skateboard, zooming up and down the drainage system, or playing video games but never like this, never doing what they were doing to him.

Not him.

Some other boy.

CHAPTER NINETEEN

AND SO A kind of awe had come to James Vachon.

He drove for Carlyle Rissden and other men who came and decided he wanted to be like them, be exactly like them.

They had . . . everything.

It was not just that they had money, or power. It was more, much more. These men who came to be picked up at the airport and driven back to the airport had it all.

Everything there was for a man, a person, a human to have—they had. They smelled of it when he picked them up, walked like it, acted like it, *breathed* like it.

They owned the world.

When they talked to him, which was rare—spoke to him to give him orders or to tip him—they *knew* they were going to be listened to, *knew* they would be heard and obeyed.

They came from all over and after several groups of them had come he realized that Rissden was in some measure like them. He was, in one way, a glorified pimp—no. The word was different. He was a solicitor for them. That was it. Not just sex, but anything they wanted.

Sometimes they came to play cards, poker, in private games for private stakes—although James guessed they were staggering. And Rissden would arrange a safe place, a house, with servants and the best of all possible foods and drink and bedrooms with women, several women, if the men wished to leave the table.

James did not know what this all cost but it didn't matter. The cost simply did not matter to them, was not part of what they thought about.

And of all things, that perhaps hit James the hardest.

He had not thought of it until he had picked up a group of three men at the airport. Many of the groups came from foreign countries—had accents he could not place. Some were oriental. But this particular party of men sounded thick somehow, had thick words—almost Russian—and as they left the airport one of them directed him to a place called Bayside Marina.

"Just drive past, please, I wish to see something."

James had done as directed and the man had ordered him to stop in front of a slip containing a single boat.

Or ship. It was huge, an enormous pleasure yacht, the kind that would take a crew of ten or twelve, plus servants. A small town, James had thought, stopping.

"I picked it up for my son," the man had said. "He's always been interested in boats."

Ahh, yes, James had thought—the boy had always been interested in boats. Of course.

As the saying goes, money was no object.

James began to understand wealth, the wealth these men had who came to be catered to by Rissden. James would sometimes lie in his apartment at night and think of it. Rissden was by no means poor —James guessed he was a multi-millionaire—but he was just rich, just had money. These other men had wealth. Rissden could own things, they could own countries, people. They could own worlds.

When Rissden lined up the special parties for them, with girls or boys—always in a different house—they were never surprised. They always seemed to expect what came to them, even the most incredible things.

They deserved it, James thought—they always seemed to think they deserved things and he wanted that feeling, that part of it more than all the rest.

To deserve all things, to have and deserve all things because of wealth—to have power and wealth and to deserve every good thing that came.

God.

It was strange. James had more than he had ever had in his life. He had a job, money to burn, a place to live and yet he wanted more, always more. When they tipped him it was always big and it always made him want more.

Rissden gave him a raise. Two hundred and fifty a week more. Just like that. And he wanted more.

And there came a day when Rissden leaned forward over the back seat and told him:

"I am increasing your area of responsibility involving certain operations."

James had nodded. "Good. I can handle it."

Although when he found what the work was he was not sure he *could* handle it.

Catering to the rich men was a complicated process. Rissden had done some of it himself—working as a chief contractor, hiring the subcontractors. James could see that Rissden always kept himself out of the picture, or almost always, working through the subcontractors but Rissden brought James in now as another buffer.

"You will get another raise of one thousand a week and you will be in charge of the entertainment," Rissden said.

Which was not what he meant, James found.

After one group had gone Rissden had sent James alone to the house to, "Clean things up. Turk will show you what to do this first time."

The "entertainment" had turned out to be a young girl. She had long, dark hair and seemed drunk, or drugged, and was lying on her side nude on a bed in the back bedroom.

James had been on the street and knew she had been used roughly, really used. But that was life. He didn't make the rules.

But he was not quite ready for the next part. Turk took a small case out of his coat pocket and removed a hypodermic needle and gave the girl a shot.

She took two long breaths and then the breathing stopped.

"She's dead." It slipped out. He had learned long before not to speak or act surprised at anything

Turk or Jared or Rissden did but it slipped out and Turk looked at him.

Just a look, no words, but James knew not to say anything else. Ever.

Turk wrapped the girl's body in a blanket. They had come to the house in the evening and they waited until it was dark, using the time to clean the rest of the house up—they threw away food and dozens of bottles of whiskey, emptied the place completely, all with the girl's body wrapped on the bed upstairs.

Finally, when it was pitch dark they put the body in the back of the car—they'd brought a Ford sedan rather than the limo—and Turk had ordered him to drive out in the country west of Boston.

James had thought they were going to find somewhere to dump the body in the woods but after driving for close to an hour they came to a dirt road off to the right and Turk told him to take it.

There were open fields on each side and farms scattered here and there—not a particularly good place to dump a body—but Turk kept him driving until they pulled around a corner and suddenly arrived at an airstrip. It was a dirt strip and seemed very short to James but before they'd been there twenty minutes a small twin-engine plane—James knew nothing of names of planes—came flying from the direction of Boston and settled gently onto the strip.

All this time Turk had been silent in the car and he now turned to James.

"You will go in the plane. When the pilot tells you, you will throw the body—just the body, not the blanket—out of the small hatch in back of the seats and then go with the pilot. You will fold the blanket and throw it in the trash wherever you land." He handed James an envelope. "Here is some money. When the pilot lands again you will take a commercial plane back to Boston. Got all that?"

It seemed insane to James. To go through all this trouble just to get rid of a body and he started to say something but changed his mind and nodded. "Yes."

It was, he knew, the way Rissden did things. When he'd taken over the chop shop he probably could have done it by just moving in—maybe some rough stuff. Instead he had killed a man, or ordered it done.

He was thorough.

If he wanted to do it this way he would do it this way and what the hell was the difference to James anyway? The pay was good—the best he'd ever had—and he'd learned long ago when to keep his mouth shut.

But he thought.

The plane stopped and wheeled around on the end of the small strip and he left Turk in the car and took the body—it was surprisingly small and light—

in the back through the small hatch and James climbed silently into the plane and moved into the back seat as Turk instructed.

The pilot sat, didn't look at him, didn't say anything.

The plane took off, climbing fast and headed east, back over Boston and all the time James thought.

To spend all this time and money just to get rid of some dead street kid, to go to this length just seemed ridiculous to him. You could have flopped her in a dumpster and nobody would have known the difference.

Insane.

To go to this length was just crazy.

They flew past Boston and out over the sea for what seemed a long time and finally the pilot said: "All right."

It was the only time he'd uttered a word and James leaned over the back seat and opened the small baggage hatch. It pulled inward and hit the foot of the body and he had to jam things around a bit. Then he slid the body out, remembering at the last minute to grab the blanket before it flopped out into the slipstream.

Then he closed the hatch and folded the blanket and sat back in the seat in silence until the pilot landed at—of all places—Ames, Iowa. There he got a shuttle, then a jet back to Boston and a cab back to

Rissden's and all the time, all the time he thought how crazy it was, how insane.

But that had been the first time. After several more—two more girls and a boy, then another boy —he realized what Rissden was doing, or more to the point, how he was doing it. He always varied the location of the party—sometimes the house in Boston, sometimes upstate New York, sometimes out west in the desert, or a house in Denver. Once up in Montana, another time in Seattle. All over the place. After breaking James in, Turk would take James with him to set things up and "clean up" afterward and they were gone at least once a month, sometimes more. The business seemed to grow. Perhaps one group of men told another, James didn't know. But the word spread and Rissden seemed to have no end of customers for his special parties.

He never allowed the bodies to be dumped in the same area as the party. Sometimes over the ocean, sometimes in the mountains, sometimes way west over the desert—always in different places.

Always the pilot would keep his head forward and say just: "All right."

And James would dump the body. It was never during daylight and he never knew where he would land. Turk gave him more than enough money for a ticket home—one time it would be Minneapolis, the next Tucson or Denver. Never the same place twice and never any tie, not the slightest link to Rissden.

Except for Turk and James.

He thought of that, too. Prison had taught him to cover his own ass—figuratively as well as literally—and he saw how easy it would be for Rissden to disassociate himself from the situation. Just remove James and the link was gone.

But as long as nothing went wrong James was safe and he'd taken more risks in his life for one hell of a lot less money.

So he did as he was told.

And thought.

Thought of how much money the men must spend, must throw to Rissden for these small, private "parties." To fly in, spend a night getting their jollies and fly out—one night and Rissden could spend the kind of money he did on "cleaning up," as he put it—they must be dumping a hundred grand and more. Maybe two hundred. Enough for Rissden to pay for all this and make a profit besides. And knowing Rissden it would be one hell of a profit.

It didn't matter to them. Money didn't matter to them. They could leave the Riviera in their jet in the morning, stop for lunch in Paris, fly to the States for the night and be back by noon the next day. They wouldn't know what came later—the body, any of it—and it probably wouldn't matter to them if they did. They hired Rissden to "clean up."

Just took what they wanted and moved on.

Class, James thought—real class. In prison

there were wolves—men who took what they wanted—and rabbits, those who got taken. James had always fallen somewhere between but he had always wanted to be a wolf.

These were the wolves. These men who came to the parties were the true wolves.

CHAPTER TWENTY

It was eleven o'clock and Tally had fallen asleep leaning back on the couch with his mouth open. When he was working his sleeping habits, all his habits became sporadic. He would eat, sleep, wherever he caught a minute. A lot of this came from covering wars, where sleep might not come for two, three days and then only in short bursts leaning against a building or in a hole.

His eyes snapped open with the sound of the phone and he flipped the switch on and raised it.

"Tyron here."

"Just a second, I'm thick." Tally opened his eyes wide, slapped his cheek. "All right."

"It seems you just can't lose me. They put me on nights and I hadn't been on two hours when we got the call. We just found Andy Kleinst."

"Found?"

"Yeah. He's in his car. I'm calling from a pay phone. Somebody professional put one in his temple. It looks like a .22 but it might be a little bigger. No witnesses, no fuss, no muss. He took it sitting and fell over against the window. Not even any blood."

"I was waiting for him to come here."

"He's not coming."

"Would it do any good for me to come down there?"

Tyron snorted. "Shit. There's about a hundred of us here now."

Tally hesitated—like all reporters he hated to give out any information. To anybody. Then he thought what the hell—Tyron had dumped it on him in the first place. "Look, Kleinst called and said he had something for me, said it was very important. See if there's anything, papers or something in his wallet that might look like he meant it for me. A name, address, anything."

"Will do."

It was so rare, this cooperation between press and police that it surprised him when Tyron agreed so readily.

"I'll call later," Tyron said.

And in truth it was not much later. Tally had just started a new pot of coffee, going under the adage that when working you could never have enough coffee, when the phone rang again.

"Bingo." It was Tyron's voice.

"What is it?"

"One of those sticky notes, folded over and stuck in his wallet with a name and time on it."

"What's the name?"

"Devon. Clair Devon. And the time written down was two o'clock."

"The Clair Devon?"

"How the hell would I know? That's all it says—isn't that enough for you?"

Tally hung up.

A woman somehow didn't fit into this—and especially not this woman.

Clair Devon was old money in Denver. Old, *big* money. She was sixty, a widow, had been born into money—money that went all the way back to the Molly Brown days and gold mining, and it was said she used her beauty like a tool to marry into even more money when she nailed Barron Devon. The Devon side of the family had money from oil. Old man Devon had bought oil rights from the Indians in Oklahoma for a nickel an acre and some corn liquor in jars and when the 1912 oil boom came, and the First World War, he couldn't bale the money fast enough to keep up.

Clair Devon had become a widow at forty, courtesy of a plane crash. She and Barron had parented three children, all sons, and the family fortune was large enough—in the billions—to provide plenty to go around. All three sons worked back into the family money but it was said that Clair ran them, ran everything with an iron hand.

Clair was almost rabidly conservative and Tally had done a story on her back in the early contra-Nicaragua days because she had given a rumored five million for guns for the contras to "stop the communists," but had spent almost as much to keep her sons out of the draft and Vietnam.

At the time she had not allowed an interview, no personal contact at all and he'd worked entirely from file information and other sources.

And here was her name in Andy's pocket.

He looked at his watch. Midnight.

He'd call her in the morning. Or try to. Right now there was time for more sleep and he didn't know when there would be another chance.

He lay back on the couch and closed his eyes and was asleep almost instantly.

Probably the single most important tool for a journalist was the telephone. When they'd blown the Watergate story open almost all the work Woodward and Bernstein did was on the phone—using one source to pop another.

It was surprisingly effective in a majority of cases but Tally was surprised that it worked with Clair.

The procedure was simple, Tally thought, making the call. You just telephoned the subject and used information as pressure.

"Hello, Mrs. Devon," Tally had said, once he got through the receptionist and secretary—which also surprised him. "My name is Janrus—yes, the reporter. Mrs. Devon, your name was found in the wallet of a Mr. Andy Kleinst who was murdered in his car last night. Would you like to comment on it?"

He was hoping for some reaction—if nothing but to hear a click as she hung up. He was almost taken aback when instead she said:

"I can give you fifteen minutes. From nine-forty-five to ten o'clock. Be here."

It had given Tally exactly twenty-one minutes to get to his Jeep, drive across town and find a parking place near the Devon building, get in and up the elevator.

He made it—with two minutes to spare—and at

precisely nine-forty-five he was ushered into Clair Devon's office.

The room was large, sparsely furnished with modern walnut and chrome office furniture. Some original modern oil paintings were on the walls and the office was located on a corner of the building with two glass walls so that it seemed to soar out over Denver.

"Mr. Janrus," she said, turning from the window. "How good of you to come."

Her voice was flat, even, powerful and left Janrus with no delusions. She was most emphatically not happy to see him.

With the window light at her back it was hard to see her well but Tally could see enough. Sixty years had not diminished her beauty. She was still extremely handsome, with a straight carriage and good figure. Her face was long with wide set, brown eyes and while her hair was gray it was still thick and rich looking, worn down in a simple cut to her shoulders.

She would live to be a hundred, Tally thought, and be beautiful when she died.

"You had something you wished to know." She said. It was not a question. A statement. Like the weather.

"Yes," Tally said. "Just as I said on the phone—a question. Do you have any idea why your name was in Andy Kleinst's pocket?"

She did not answer immediately, but paused, thinking. One long finger rubbing her temple. God, Tally thought, she is the most beautiful woman I have ever seen. A sixty-year-old Nefertiti.

"Kleinst is—was the lowest of slime, Mr. Janrus," she said, finally. "Surely you knew that."

Tally nodded. "He was not somebody I would invite to the prom—still, your name was there."

She did not smile. "I have absolutely no idea why my name was in his pocket. . . ."

"Name and time." Tally interrupted. A little push now, a nudge. "Like appointment time."

She shrugged. "I still have no idea. I most certainly did not have an appointment with him."

"A guess." Tally said. "Could you make an educated guess as to his reason for having your name?"

Again the pause, thinking. She never said anything unplanned, Tally thought, nothing spontaneous, nothing in anger. Thought. Jesus, no wonder she was so rich—she did not know how to lose.

"There are certain people who think the rich are vulnerable," she said. "Perhaps Mr. Kleinst was one of them. He may have thought he could use some information he had to get money from me—isn't that what he was known for?"

Tally said nothing. It didn't matter what she said because she controlled the words too much. Nothing useful would come. The second question had just hit him. Why am I here, he thought suddenly. She didn't let me come here to tell me anything.

She wants to know if I know anything. That's it. She wants to find out what I know. That's why she let me come here. So there is something going on—goddamn. Andy had something. He looked at his watch. Six minutes left. Well, hell, let's take a shot. Make it vague. His mind raced, trying to get ahead of the situation. She would not have done anything Andy could write about. It would have been her company—no, her family. The sons.

One of the sons.

Jesus—one of the sons was involved in this other thing with the kids?

"It would not have to be about you," Tally said. "It could be about somebody close to you."

There was some indication. A movement in the left eyebrow. The light was still wrong for Tally to be sure but he sensed it, felt it. The reaction was there. It was the sons, or one of them.

"Your time is up," she said, still not moving, standing in the light from the windows, owning the room, the building, her life. "I'm sorry I couldn't be of more help."

Dismissed, Tally thought, and he left.

CHAPTER TWENTY-ONE

BILLEE PUT THE phone back on the hook and thought about what to wear. Appearance was always important—there was some style to consider—but the clothes also had to fit the occasion. He had just called the man in Boston and told him he would be seeing to the delivery of the next package to the airstrip in New Mexico in six or seven hours.

Something functional, he thought, functional and understated—efficient outdoors business.

He put on chino pants, two-toned oxfords, an open khaki shirt with a sleeveless pastel green tee shirt beneath it.

It was dark—ten o'clock—but to top off the ensemble he put on a pair of expensive mirror sunglasses.

This was perversely the part of business he considered the most dangerous and the part he loved the best. There was such a thrill to it, such a wild thrill.

He had to go get the product and take it to Jimmy at the plane and in all of it, all the travel and contacts there was danger, real danger and he felt his breath come faster with the heat, the wild heat of it.

He decided to take the Camaro and when he drove away from the house he watched the mirror carefully, tipping the glasses momentarily up on his forehead for clear vision—Sean Connery in *From Russia with Love*—and drove around a block twice to make certain he wasn't tailed.

The place where the transfer of the product would occur was already established.

The Rev—God, Billee thought, wasn't he just the biggest country schmuck of all times?—had called and said the boy was ready.

Billee's only part in this was administrative. He had started the whole operation, working with the brute from the east—he had no names, knew nothing of what happened later and didn't want to know. The man from the east—Billie thought of him as the Hulk—had only contacted him once personally, saying that a friend of a friend of a friend had mentioned him, and told him about the money involved in finding the product. The instructions were simple: get the product to a small airstrip in New Mexico any way he could and he would be paid.

Billee knew a pilot who had run drugs and was available—for anything—and knew the Rev from past parties and it was a simple matter to bring it all together.

For a time he toyed with the idea of not being involved at all. He made a point of never touching the product, never using it himself—though he loved boys, young boys—and he thought how perfect it would be if he just remained the hidden master, the omnipotent being who controlled the whole operation.

But he knew he would lose if he took himself out of the loop. (He loved that phrase—ever since Ollie used it in his hearings. In and out of the loop. It was beautiful.) Soon the Rev would deal directly with the pilot and before Billee knew it he would be squeezed out.

But by putting himself in the loop he was exposing himself to danger and he wanted to minimize that as much as possible. It was, after all, a continuing business and if he were exposed it would stop the business. It was only natural for him to remain protected—the way generals had to be protected in war to keep things moving.

He decided that the safest place for him to enter the chain was simply to transport the product from the Rev to the plane. The time varied, but never over a couple of hours and he was done, yet it was critical. It allowed him complete control and separated the Rev from the pilot and prevented any linkup nicely.

Still, there was danger.

Which of course thrilled him. The danger of having the product in his car, driving to the plane. All he had to do was get a speeding ticket, have an accident.

Great risk.

He drove around another block, watching the mirror and when it was clear he headed for the meeting place.

Rev had most of the risk. He had to bring the boy up to San Diego for the transfer point—a long drive with crowded roads. From the transfer place to the airstrip was thirty-five miles and mostly on quiet roads, heading east and south of Los Angeles.

It took Billee just over an hour to get there and he saw that the Rev's car was already there. Billee moved the transfer each time and this time he'd selected an alley in an old section of town. The area was in back of an abandoned gas station and covered with overgrowth and climbing vines.

The Rev had backed into the alley, as instructed, and Billee drove past once, went around the block to make certain he wasn't being followed —you couldn't be too careful—and backed the Camaro into the alley in front of the Rev. Ready for a quick getaway.

The Rev got out, walked to the Camaro. Billee left his sunglasses down to obscure his face in case anybody was watching.

"You got the money?"

"Bring the product first," Billee said.

"Sure. He's on drugs but he's in good shape and well broke in. . . ."

"Let me see him."

Rev went back to the passenger side of his car and opened it and lifted a small form out, set the boy on his feet.

Davey could walk, but only barely, weaving from side to side. Billee saw that he was smiling but his eyes wobbled.

"How much has he had?"

"Don't worry," Rev said, bringing Davey to the Camaro. "She's a nurse and knows what she's doing. She didn't O.D. him."

"Put him in the car."

Rev put Davey in the passenger seat of the Camaro and strapped him in tightly. He handed a small plastic tube with a hypodermic needle inside it to Billee. "In an hour-and-a-half you can give him this and it will keep him in happy land for another five or six hours."

Davey sat quietly, grinning, staring out the window but seeing nothing. His head wobbled a bit but Billee agreed that he didn't look too bad. Not roughed up. One of the girls had been roughed up.

"Here's the money." Billee handed Rev an envelope and before he could open it put the Camaro in drive and pulled away. Not fast, sane and easy—he didn't want to attract any attention.

Everything was moving well and he drove back towards the city until he found the right off-ramp to head east.

There were orange and lemon orchards and he opened the window slightly to get the smell of the trees in to carry away the smog. It was all stink, Los Angeles, yellow stink. He was slightly above it where he lived but not much and when he drove down and through the city sometimes it almost gagged him.

He looked at the boy who had fallen asleep—or into a drug daze. His head was over against the door of the car and Billee had to admit that Rev knew how to pick them. The boy was gorgeous, with soft blond hair and wide blue eyes and Billee had a moment of sadness thinking that it was a sacrifice to remove himself so much from the action. He would have liked to turn the boy out—he had not done it for some time. Not since the last street boy he'd done years before, before AIDS. He was sure the boy was new—of course the little shit could have been lying to him—and it was so deliciously wicked to show the boy the world as it really was. . . . ahh, those days were gone. AIDS had ruined it all.

Davey made a sound, a deep breath, almost a moan. Probably a dream. Billee reached over to make sure he was still strapped in all right, then went back to driving.

Someday, Billee thought, someday he'll think back on this time and love it; he'll remember it as his turning-out time and memorize each moment. Just as Billee had done. With Billee it had been an uncle, Uncle Buser. Billee's parents had been gone for the day and Uncle Buser was visiting and had found him—twelve years old—playing in his room. It had been a wonderful afternoon and he remembered each moment of it, each time of it, each position of it though there had been a million moments, a thousand times and a thousand positions since.

This boy would be the same. He would remember all this with happiness.

He wondered what the boy's name was—mentally kicked himself for not asking Rev. Maybe Johnny. He looked like a Johnny.

Billee drove well out into the country until he reached a gravel sideroad that moved off the narrow asphalt roadway to the south. He took the gravel, slowing.

The sudden bumpiness awakened the boy and he looked up, his eyes still glazed. He said something but it didn't make sense, just sound, and Billee looked at his watch.

Another thirty minutes and he could give the shot.

Except that he was due at the plane soon and he didn't like to delay—he didn't want to wait until enough time had gone by to give the next shot, sit there, exposed. Things had to be kept moving.

He stopped the car and made certain there were no other vehicles on the narrow road. He'd have to give the boy a partial shot, enough to hold him until he reached New Mexico.

Billee turned on the dome light and examined the hypodermic. The boy squinted in the sudden light and mumbled something.

Half. He'd give him half. Hopefully it wouldn't be enough to kill him but would still keep him under until he was delivered.

He raised the boy's tee shirt sleeve and quickly gave him the shot, holding back even still more so that only about a third of the drug went into the arm.

It would have to do. Billee was afraid to give more. Drugs were tricky. They'd overdosed a girl early on, when they first started the business before the Rev had tied up with the nurse, and she had died.

No cars had come and he turned the light off and drove again. In ten minutes he came to another side road, a twin rut, and he took this, the headlights bouncing off orange trees on the sides of the road until, finally, he stopped before a long clearing. He turned off his lights and waited, the engine idling.

He had been early, but in just moments and before he really had time to think he saw the Cessna 210 settle onto the grass strip in the moonlight and taxi to the car.

Billee could almost smell the mystery and intrigue. Planes landing in the night, packages exchanging hands—or people. It was all so . . . so Second World War-ish.

He opened the door, walked around and took the boy out and carried him to the plane.

Billee met the pilot—Jimmy Willems—back when he'd played for a time with drugs, before he'd decided it was much too dangerous. Not because of the law but because of the other drug people. They had no rules and there was so *much* money—one didn't know when they would decide to just cut you in little pieces and kill you. Completely unpredictable.

The business of entertainment products made less money but was far safer. There weren't Colombians hiding under every bush waiting to take a chain saw to your neck.

Jimmy had flown drugs then and when Billee contacted him about entertainment he agreed readily and smiled as Billee strapped the boy in the back seat and dropped the front seat back into position.

He also wore mirrored sunglasses and Billee could see the reflections of his glasses in the pilot's glasses.

"Right on time," Billee said over the sound of the idling engine, nodding his approval. "So professional. . . ."

"We aim to please." Jimmy spoke almost entirely in clichés.

"Same place in New Mexico," Billee said. "I just gave him a shot so he should be all right for several hours."

"With these winds I should be there in four, maybe four-and-a-half hours."

"You'll be fine. . . ."

He handed the pilot an envelope with money in it and the pilot stuck it on a clipboard which was attached to his knee. Billee always paid up front.

He watched the plane turn, bouncing on the grass. Jimmy had full flaps down and when he gunned the engine the Cessna seemed almost to bounce into the air.

Billee watched it leave. When it was well up,

above the trees and climbing for altitude the lights came on.

He felt almost let down. There had been the danger, the fear of exposure, a sense of heightened excitement and it was gone now. His part was done and there was a kind of sadness.

Well, almost done.

There was the money yet. That was something still to do. The man in Boston would have to send the money.

But there was little risk in that.

CHAPTER TWENTY-TWO

TALLY LOOKED AT the papers on the coffee table and wondered if it could really be that easy.

As soon as he left Clair Devon he went to the office of the *Star.* He knew a reporter there who owed him some favors and he spent the rest of the day going through their files and copying anything remotely associated with the Devons—specifically the sons.

There were three of them. Two of them had gone to college, come home, stepped into the business and settled into expanding the family fortune and getting richer.

The third one—named Brice—had proven to be a bit more active. He had done college as well—they'd all gone to Harvard—but somewhere along the line had become an even more rabid conservative than his mother. Clair was conservative only inasmuch as it served her—like many rich people. Brice had gone off the deep end.

He joined every right-wing organization that came along, worked on political campaigns for the far, far, far right—what Tally thought of as baby Nazis.

There were quotes:

"People who burn the flag should be shot for treason."

"Doctors who perform abortions should be executed for murder."

"Women are meant for home and breeding." (That one, Tally thought, must have gone over well with his mother.)

"There should be camps for malcontents."

"All Hitler's policies weren't bad."

He had proven to be a handful for his mother, who apparently spent a great deal of money trying to tone his image down and after a time Brice had settled.

At least externally—publicly. But he had not changed and he became involved, almost as a natural flow, in the running of guns to the contras and other groups in Central America and was associated with ex-professional soldiers—Green Berets, ex-Delta Force personnel, mercenaries.

Men, Tally thought, who could put a bullet in Andy Kleinst's head and walk away.

But none of this would have any bearing on Andy's death were it not for the other side of Brice.

Large amounts of money had been spent to hide the fact that Brice liked strange sex. He had married and divorced three times, all divorces under a cloud —the wives apparently roughly used, paid off to keep quiet. One of the wives possibly suffered brain damage. He had not remarried after the third one but had been caught twice in Denver with male prostitutes—both young boys. The information was in the file but had not been published. There was also an incident in Washington at a male house of prostitution where a reporter had followed a raid in and caught Brice with a young congressional page. Again, the information was in the "quiet" file—background studies—but no story had been published. Or at least no story with Brice.

Kill fees.

Andy Kleinst.

Tally rubbed his eyes with a thumb and index

finger. He had been reading for five solid hours and they were burning.

The facts were a little rubbery but almost no journalistic truth could be found in raw facts. Stories were always more complicated, more hidden than that. Facts led to ideas, and ideas to extrapolation—lines that went out from the facts and led to truth.

And this story was ripe for extrapolating.

Andy must have gone to Brice Devon for a kill fee. Say it had worked the first time. Brice had paid him off—or perhaps mother had paid Andy off. Whatever. So Brice had contacts all over the place and he'd found that Tally was working on the story and had told Andy to warn Tally off.

It hadn't worked.

But was that enough reason to kill Andy?

It all seemed weak to Tally.

Unless you factored in Andy Kleinst's greed. Say Andy went back. He'd tapped the mother lode, found that Brice Devon had something to do with the dead kid and decided to go back for more money.

Brice had somebody punch Andy's ticket and that was that.

Not quite.

There was Tally.

If Brice had taken Andy out for the story, had

used his contacts to get Mel Tyron off the case—if it was worth all that he would also move against Tally.

Except that he hadn't.

Tally leaned back. There had been plenty of time for some reaction and nothing had come.

He rose and went to the bedroom, opened the closet. From the top shelf of the closet he took a box and opened it.

It contained a nine millimeter automatic—a Smith and Wesson—with two extra clips and a back belt holster. He made certain the clips were full and slipped one in the gun, locked it in place and jacked the slide back to push a shell into the chamber. Then he eased the hammer forward and put the safety on and slid the holster over his belt in the small of his back.

Tally had long ago decided against passive journalism. He knew many—most—journalists would not arm themselves. There was the thought that if you were armed you became too much a part of the story. Also there was the feeble hope that if you were not armed you would be elevated above the action and would be safe. Or at least partially safe.

Which Tally knew was bullshit. In Central America they used reporters—as well as priests, nuns and social workers—for target practice.

So he armed himself. And he practiced. He worked the police range every three months or so, dumped three or four boxes through the nine millimeter until he passed police qualification. He had a permit.

And he had used the gun.

He had a rule—a rough rule he followed. When, or more importantly, *if* the story developed in such a way as to make him an active part in it—if, for instance, Brice or somebody he hired made a move against Tally, a physical move—Tally would remove that part of the story that involved him.

He did not write about that aspect of it when he covered the story, never brought himself into it personally, but there had been several occasions when it became necessary to protect himself—or as he thought of it, insure his clinical detachment from the story—and he had not hesitated to do it.

He knew journalists who did not and some of them, a good many of them were dead.

"You must eat the bear," a drill instructor had told him as a recruit, "before the son of a bitch eats you."

And so the gun.

He went back into the living room and as he entered the room noticed the phone machine. He'd been so involved with the papers and work when he came in that he hadn't thought to check for messages.

There were two—the light blinked twice, then stopped. Blinked again.

He hit the switch.

"Tyron here. Give me a call when you can. I'll be at work. Forever."

There was a moment of silence, then the second call.

It was Kari. Her voice had an edge to it—she was irritated. "I got your message, Tal, but I must say I'm not pleased that you had a friend call. It seems like you could have just as easily called yourself."

Kari, he thought.

They hit me there—Kari.

He grabbed the phone and dialed her number.

CHAPTER TWENTY-THREE

DAVEY COULD ALMOST literally feel the drug wear off. It was like diving in the pool and coming up from the bottom slowly with your eyes open.

At first it was dark and blue and everything was all funny and screwy. Faces moved on people's heads, wobbled and wiggled and the eyes would droop or the ears could hang like dog's ears and almost everything made him laugh.

He knew where he was but it was all a dream, too, so he couldn't draw the line where real things ended and dream things began. He remembered the house, and the terrible things the man and woman did to him, but sometimes they were like they had happened to other people, some other boy and Davey had only been watching from the corner of the room.

Then that memory would drop and he would remember the car ride and looking out the window at all the orange trees as they whizzed past, all a blur in the moonlight.

And he remembered the man, the men. The big man called Rev who had done all the bad things to him and the woman he remembered and he sort of remembered the man in the car driving him through all the orange trees.

And he remembered the shot. The man in the car had given him a shot and everything had become all funny again so he couldn't remember the rest of the ride through the oranges.

Or how he got into an airplane.

He was in an airplane now, sitting strapped into the back seat and he could not remember getting into an airplane or taking off.

The pilot sat up front on the left side and he was flying with his hands lightly on the controls.

An airplane.

Davey shook his head. Things were still funny,

upside down, and he thought he might be dreaming the plane but he was getting closer to the top of the pool, closer to the surface all the time and the airplane was still there.

And he was still flying in it, sitting in the back seat.

He had stopped smiling. His head hurt and he had a gummy taste in his mouth and when the funny parts left he was scared.

Memories rushed back and he made a sound, a small cry—it was hard not to cry—but the sound of the plane engine was loud and the pilot did not hear him, did not look back.

How long?

How long had it been since the big man named Rev talked him into following him to the car?

He could not tell, not even guess. Two days, four days, a week, a month—he didn't know. There had been food. What was that? Pizza. Lots of pizza and Coke—that's all they fed him.

And the shots. Davey knew about drugs—any kid on the street in San Diego knew about drugs. He had even tried a joint once when he was small that some punk geek at the high school gave him.

But this was different.

Some wild kind of drug that made his arms hang at his side and everything all crazy and wobbly.

But it was wearing off now.

He could move his arms and he raised his hands and looked at them and they did not look funny. They were his hands, not claws or colored hooks or paws with snaky fingers. They were his hands.

He moved his feet. Slowly, carefully because he didn't want the pilot to look back. His legs worked, everything worked. He was stiff and he hurt but all the parts worked and he thought what he would do if this were a movie.

If it were all a movie and not real he would take something heavy and hit the pilot on the head and take over the plane and land at the nearest airport and he would be safe.

Safe.

But this wasn't a movie. It wasn't a drug dream and it wasn't a movie and he was really sitting in a real plane and there was a real pilot and he was flying through the night.

The pilot turned and looked at him but Davey kept his head down and let it wiggle a little bit and the pilot turned back.

Davey's thinking was coming back as well and he tried to think of a way out. He had to get away but how could he get away when he was strapped in an airplane flying?

He'd wait.

The plane had to come down sometime, land some place. He didn't know but he thought small planes like this didn't carry a lot of gas and would have to come down before too long.

Out the window he could see lights. City lights off to the right and left, thousands of lights and he thought that where all those lights were there would also be people. All those people just doing what they did with their lives and not knowing he was flying over them in a small airplane. How could they not know it?

If he could just get to the people, any people, they would help him.

He'd wait and pretend to still be feeling the drugs and as soon as he got a chance he would run. He would run like his legs had never run before—break and run and run and run.

He would wait.

CHAPTER TWENTY-FOUR

MARTIN WAITED IN the desert night and thought that the only good thing that came with age was a certain amount of patience.

The drug planes would come. Or they would not come. Sometimes he thought it didn't make any difference and the only thing that counted was the waiting. Life was all waiting. Except for the pain and the money he needed to stop the pain it did not matter one way or the other.

There had been many desert nights such as this when he was young. Cool, almost cold with some sharp edges in the air and he had spent them watching over herds of sheep in the high country before bringing them down. Or he had spent them with the girls from town when he was young and they would come out to his camp and spend the night hours beneath his blankets to warm him.

There was that about age as well—memories. Flat stomachs and firm breasts and soft laughter under the blankets and promises.

Promises.

It would all last forever then, in the memories. It would all last forever and there would never be age or aching bones or the silliness of waiting for the drug planes.

He added a piece of pinion to the fire. He had debated with himself a long time about the fire so close to the place where the planes came to land. But it was fall now and the nights were cold and he finally decided to allow himself only a small fire to make the ache go away. He made the fire in a hole in the ground and had a mound of loose sand that he could kick over the flames when the airplanes came.

Not if.

When.

He was sure they would come because he

needed them to come so that he could get the money for the expensive drugs and so they would come.

He dozed for a time but he did not worry that he would sleep too hard. He never slept hard now—just dozed in small fits. Like a dog sleeping with his legs jerking at the dreams. That's how he slept. Or did not sleep.

Old dogs and old men have nothing but their dreams, he thought, eyes half-closed and the flames warming his face. They are good dreams and maybe they were enough—the dreams.

Perhaps there will be money in the planes as well, he thought. There would be the reward but there might be money in the planes and if there was enough money perhaps he could afford one of the young women who sold themselves in Santa Fe.

He would rent a room in the motel with the large bird in front on the sign and the girl would stay with him the whole night and he would not be old for that time and he let his memories mix with the fantasies until he felt even his old guts tighten with the thoughts.

Stupido.

Muy stupido.

To lie and dream by the fire about things that could never be. Even if there was money there could not be young women. He was too old for that.

He moved the rifle next to him, eased his position. There was that, he knew.

There was always the rifle and he wondered why he had not done it? He did not believe in the shit of the church that said it was wrong to end yourself. He had long before decided that the church was all shit. That all churches were all shit.

Still.

There was some small thing from his youth that kept him from putting the barrel of the rifle in his mouth and saying to hell with all the pain and silliness. Some small thing that would not let him do it.

But it was probably the easiest way. There was nothing for him now but the end anyway. A time with the drugs to stop the pain in his joints and then there would be another time in the state home and then there would be nothing for him.

It would be the same for him as it had been for Carlos Romero. Carlos was the same age as Martin except that something had gone wrong in his brain and one side of his face did not work and he could not think straight. Martin smiled. It was not that Carlos could *ever* think straight. But when Carlos' face stopped working they put him in the home and Martin went to see him one time because they had spent much of their youth together, shared bottles and women and nights on the desert.

They had Carlos tied in a bed and he did not see Martin or hear Martin or know that Martin had come to visit him. While Martin was there they came to feed Carlos. They pushed a plastic plunger in his mouth and jammed something that looked like baby shit down Carlos' throat and that was his meal.

So sometimes the rifle did not look so bad even if there was this problem from his youth that kept him from shooting himself.

He dozed again, in and out of it and thought that if the planes did not come this night perhaps he would honor the rifle and was thinking that, wondering what would be the best way to do this thing when he heard the sound of the plane engine.

CHAPTER TWENTY-FIVE

THE PROBLEM, JAMES thought, was in getting Turk to talk.

In all the work they'd done for Rissden Turk didn't talk to James except to give him instructions.

Come to that, none of them did. Rissden only spoke when he gave an order and Jared never spoke to him at all and it was starting to worry James.

Especially now.

It had been a beautiful fall day, sunny and cool in the morning and he'd had a breakfast at a nearby cafe and come back ready to work.

Except when he reported in there had been something in the air. Normally he went to Rissden's office in the big house—there was a back door used as a working entrance—and received the orders for the day. And this morning he'd done that, entering without knocking—he felt that he was becoming more and more a part of what was going on—and had walked into a problem.

There was a small entry alcove before the doorway to Rissden's office and James usually stopped there and waited to be called into the large, carpeted study that was the office proper.

The door was open and he realized that Rissden had not heard him come in.

He was speaking to Turk.

". . . there is a rough spot in Denver which could come back at us. Perhaps it is best to detach at this time. There's no sense being greedy. See to it."

Which might not have been that much of a problem. Except.

Except that they had recently done a party in Denver. Or, more accurately, in a suburb in the mountains near Denver at a large home and James had thought it had gone very well. They had dumped the body in the mountains and James had flown home from Albuquerque and nobody had said anything about any "rough spots."

Except that he knew something of how Rissden "detached" from things because he'd been with the organization long enough now to have seen it happen.

The chop shop incident was fresh in his mind. The little popping sound and watching the man drop would never leave his memory.

And finally there was the knowledge that he was the only real attachment between Rissden and the whole business of the parties. Rissden himself never saw the pilot—only Turk and James. Not even Jared was involved in that part of it. And on most of the last ones—the party in Denver, for instance—only James had been involved.

He had thought it was because he was becoming more and more trusted, allowed more and more responsibility in the organization but there was the other side of it as well.

He was the only attachment.

And there was an unpleasant sound to *de*tachment.

He had reopened the front door and closed it loudly and they had stopped talking.

"Come in, James," Rissden had said. "We have another party tomorrow."

"Where is it?"

"In Chicago. The item to be picked up will be in

New Mexico. You will fly to Albuquerque tonight and meet the plane there, then proceed to Chicago."

James nodded.

"Oh—I almost forgot to mention. Turk will be accompanying you on this one. There are some other things to take care of and he must see to them. He has the address of the place in Chicago."

"Sure. Fine."

So in the late afternoon he and Turk had driven to the airport and booked coach flights to New Mexico and Turk had settled his bulk into the small seat and in all of that time had not said one word.

Not a word.

And James wished he would talk.

He had tried to draw the big man out, get him into a conversation but Turk only nodded and stared out the window. When the stewardess came James ordered a bourbon and water but Turk took nothing except a cup of tea which he ordered with one word.

"Tea."

"Sugar or cream?" The stewardess had asked.

Turk shook his head.

One word.

When they landed at Albuquerque Turk had rented a car to drive to the small plane strip to meet Aaron and on the way he had gone to a sporting goods store.

"Wait here," he'd told James and left him in the car.

He'd come out in twenty minutes and settled back into the car and when his coat opened James had seen a small handgun at his belt on his left side.

Pop.

He could not have brought it on the plane but there were no rules in New Mexico, Texas, Arizona —no waiting rules so he could buy one right away.

"What did you do?" James had asked but Turk had just shaken his head, said nothing.

Detachment, James thought. Pop. Detachment.

It was strange. Part of him, an inner part was becoming frantic with worry. But on the outside he was calm, collected, waiting for an opportunity. There was nothing sure yet but he had to cover himself.

Life came that way, he knew. Came with luck and no luck. If he hadn't walked into the alcove without knocking, if the door hadn't been opened to Rissden's office he wouldn't have heard anything and he wouldn't know what was coming.

But that little thing, that simple thing had happened and now he knew and could take steps to save himself. Luck.

They drove to the small strip—or actually large one. It had been a training airstrip during the Second World War and had huge, largely empty hangars and revetments. Since closing down in the sixties it had become a general-use airfield for private and small planes and it was where they were to meet Aaron and the twin-engine Bonanza.

It was eight o'clock when they arrived and dark enough to see stars. They were still many hours early—they weren't to meet Aaron until well after midnight.

They pulled up in the parking lot which was poorly lighted and empty except for some dusty cars that had obviously been there for a time.

"We'll sleep," Turk said—his voice cracking the silence in the car. "By the time we fly to Chicago it will be a long night."

James nodded. "Yeah. But I'm hungry."

"You ate on the plane."

"Right," James snorted. "Get serious."

"You'll live."

"Maybe we could go back into town and get a burger or something."

"Too many people to see," Turk said, slouching back and down in the driver's seat and leaning his head against the window. "You'll live."

That, thought James, is exactly what I'm worried about.

Detachment.

Pop.

CHAPTER TWENTY-SIX

TIME, TALLY THOUGHT.

It all came down to time.

His body wanted to run, to smash something and run to Kari's ranch stop . . . whatever was going to happen.

But that would take time. An hour plus. Too long. He would go there but he had to stabilize the situation first.

When had she called? She had not said the time.

Maybe she was still there, still all right.

He rang her number, let it ring ten times, fifteen times. No answer.

He switched the phone off. Think. He couldn't make his mind think.

Tyron.

He called the police station, was put on hold, fumed and, finally, Tyron came on.

"What's up?"

"It's me. They're moving against me. The same people who hit Andy Kleinst."

"How?" Tyron's voice was clipped, official.

Quickly Tally told what had happened, all of it, down to his deduction that it was Brice Devon Andy was working on and about the fake telephone message on Kari's machine.

Tyron whistled softly through his teeth. "He has heavy friends."

"I need help. Now."

Tyron thought a moment. "I'll call the sheriff's department out there—she's in Packer County, isn't she?"

"Yes."

"They can get there quicker than anybody."

"I'll start driving now—tell them to hurry."

He turned the phone off and threw it on the couch, ran for the door.

Old tapes played while he drove.

There could be nobody—you could have nobody if you did this great whore, the whore of finding the story. There were too many ways to be hurt, too many people to be hurt.

To love, to have what he had with Kari made him weak, put her in terrible danger and made him weak and he knew a terrible loss. Even if she was all right he had lost. He had tried this one time, one more time, tried to be normal and it hadn't worked and would never work, never work. . . .

The Jeep screamed down the freeway. At Castle Rock he turned off, headed west. He did not dare look at his watch.

What would it take to hurt her?

A moment. Part of a moment.

And he was driving, mile after mile, out through Elizabeth, Kiowa and finally to the turn to Kari's ranch. Taking forever, for-goddamn-*ever* to move, to get there.

A mile from the house he came over a low rise and saw the buildings in the late evening night. There were lights in the house but it hadn't become dark enough to trigger the yard light yet.

He saw Kari's pickup.

There were no other vehicles.

No sheriff's car.

Nothing.

He wheeled into the yard and stepped out of the Jeep, keeping the body of the car between himself and the house.

Some birds sang, a horse stamped in the corral in back of the barn.

The automatic was in his hand, a round chambered, the hammer back.

"Kari?"

Nothing, no answer.

He moved towards the house on the outsides of his feet, waiting for some movement, some sound.

The kitchen door was open, the screen closed. He heard music now, faint strains of some country and western song.

Kari hated country and western.

He slipped through the door, easing the screen shut in back of him.

The music was louder now. Willie Nelson. From upstairs, the upstairs bedroom.

He paused for a second at the bottom of the stairs. They were old and creaked and he tried to remember which steps were worst and then thought to hell with it. If somebody was up there they knew he was here, knew he was coming in.

So give it to him.

He took a breath, tensed and sprang up the steps to the bedroom door, hit it with a shoulder and knocked it in, fell in and down to the left with the automatic out in front held in both hands, ready.

Kari was there. Alone.

She was on the bed, tied with her arms and legs spread. She was nude and her head was raised and she was making muffled sounds because her mouth was covered with duct tape.

Tally scanned the room once, saw nobody else and stood. He lay the automatic next to her on the bed and carefully removed the tape. It stuck and he worked it gently away from her skin and all the while she lay looking up at him, her big eyes looking up at him with silent tears pouring from them and he hated himself.

"There was a man," she said, as soon as the tape was off and while Tally untied her arms and legs. "There was a big man and he came and. . . ."

"Easy, easy." He held her while she cried, rocking back and forth.

". . . and he touched me and played with me and made me—made me do things. . . ."

"It's all right, it's all right."

"No. It isn't all right. A man came and he did these things to me and said to ask you about it . . . and it is *not* all right. What was he talking about, Tal? What was he *talking* about?"

But she didn't want an answer and he knew it, wanted only silence and to be comforted and when it was done, when it was all done and she had time to think she would want Tally out of her life, out and gone. And he understood that. He agreed with it. He must be out of her life. He must be out of all lives but his own. He knew that now.

There was nothing to say.

While he was holding her and she cried, burning off the fear and anger, Tally heard an engine and saw the sheriff's car coming up the driveway from the county road.

He could not have been any help even if he had come sooner. Nor could Tally. It was all done long ago, long before Tally had come into Kari's life, long before he'd even known her—all done back when he accepted the great whore of the story.

Nobody could help and there was nothing to say.

So he held her and rocked with her and felt a great loss, the greatest loss of his life and looked out the window at the prairie and tried not to think, not to know things, but just to be.

Just to sit and hold her for this time and be with her.

CHAPTER TWENTY-SEVEN

He scooped sand on the fire and it died instantly, even the smoke held down. Martin had been partially in his old sleeping bag and he pushed it off now and rose to his knees.

He was fully dressed—as he was almost always fully dressed since becoming old—and he took the rifle.

He hands hurt with the night cold, worse now

that even the small heat from the little fire was gone but he held the rifle well enough and moved towards the airstrip in the darkness.

He had no light, no flashlight, but he knew there could be no light anyway or the pilots would see it and not land and it did not matter.

He knew the desert, had been of the desert so long that he knew where things would be the way a man who had lived in a house all his life knew where things were in the house.

This hummock held the plant with the dry bean pods that rattled like a snake, over here some cactus, a dry stream bed on his right—he moved through them easily, stooped with age and the nine pounds of the rifle.

The sound of the plane engine grew louder and passed over him once but it did not have lights on and Martin moved beneath some small brush and could not be seen even in broad daylight, let alone the middle of the night.

This was the plane with two engines and he knew there would be the other one, the smaller plane.

He supposed there was logic to this thing, some logic. Perhaps the drugs came in the large plane and the smaller plane came to get them which would mean the smaller plane would have the money.

He did not count on the money and thought that the reward would be enough to get him the medicines but if he could get the money it would be nice.

The plane flew low over the runway one more time and then rose and circled and still Martin did not worry. They had done this before and he knew it was just caution and they had not seen him.

How things had changed, he thought. He found a place near the end of the runway and settled back under some mesquite on a mound of sand and rock. He was slightly higher than the strip and perhaps fifty yards from where they had stopped the last time. He eased the bolt back and made certain there was a shell in the chamber and that the clip was full. Five bullets. Five of the big bullets he had bought the time the bear were killing sheep in the mountains and he needed the big bullets to stop the bear.

Everything had changed.

He and Carlos used to sit and drink red wine and thought how strange it was when cars first came to Tres Piños and now there were planes full of drugs and money landing in the dark.

Carlos would have laughed to see such things and Martin found himself smiling though his joints hurt more and more with the cold.

He had some of the brown cloth gloves but they made his hands slippery and he did not want to risk dropping the rifle or slipping on the bolt.

It would take more than one shot to stop the engines on the planes and to get the big reward he felt he had to stop them both and he would have to shoot fast.

He put the rifle across his knees and put both hands inside his coat and was just thinking a small prayer that it would not take long for the second plane to come when he heard the new engine, coming low and from the south and knew that the waiting was over.

CHAPTER TWENTY-EIGHT

IT COULD BE done on the phone but he wanted to see the bastard's face—Tally wanted it certain.

He had taken Kari to the hospital and waited with her, sat with her through the night though they didn't talk. A barrier had already come between them and he sat with her as a friend, a good friend, but nothing more and he would never be more to her again. She was not injured except for a rash from the tape over her mouth but the doctor gave her a sedative and she slept finally, the way a small girl sleeps. Her hands clenched in tight little fists, the corners of her eyes tight and pinched.

He called Tyron while she was sleeping.

"It's Brice," he said. "Brice all the way. The son of a bitch sent one of his assholes but it was him."

"Shit. . . ." Tyron hesitated. "It's not technically in our jurisdiction but somebody will have to ask her questions, show her pictures—you know."

"It won't do any good."

"I agree. But it has to be done. I can offer you some other help, though. Do you want some protection for her?"

Tally watched a nurse move down the corridor with a tray of small plastic cups full of pills. It was two in the morning but he felt wide awake. None of the fuzz. "Everything I can get. But it won't be long. Just until I settle this thing."

"What are you going to do?"

"Do you really want to know?"

Tyron held for a moment, then sighed. "No. I'll have an officer there in ten minutes."

He called the night desk at the *Star* and got lucky. The woman working the desk was named Herron and he knew her well; tough, one of those people who always went to the center of the story no matter how hard it was, how bad it was; a practitioner of the old adage you had to get close to get true.

She gave him Brice's address from the file—he didn't want to go home and get it—and as soon as a uniformed officer arrived he made certain Kari was all right and sleeping soundly and left.

There was a great peace in him now that at first he didn't understand. He drove easily, almost slowly, not particularly caring what was coming and decided it was that he had made the decision to be alone.

There was this business to take care of, and he would do it, but if he made it through all of this he knew that he would be alone the rest of his life and somehow that settled him.

He almost didn't feel anger.

The Brice Devons of the world would always be assholes and there would always be Brice Devons so settling this didn't make much sense except for revenge. He told himself it was to insure that Kari would not be bothered again but it was not that. She was safe now. The police would protect her. If Brice moved it would be against Tally himself and after tonight he would not be able to do that.

But that wasn't why Tally was going. It wasn't anger and it wasn't revenge.

It was more. In all the time in all the places where he had seen all the goddamn Brice Devons doing what the sons of bitches did, in all the countries with all the little dictators and all the provinces in all the backwater dumps with all the little goddamn warlords and thugs sucking on the little plants of power—in all of that he had remained separate, aloof.

The journalist. *No.* The Journalist.

He had never become involved except to do the story. Get close and do the work but stay detached.

That was over now.

He thought of the boy driven into the earth and all the other boys and girls they had found and Kari, sweet Kari who had been such a clear spot in his life, wonderful Kari and knew it was over now.

The detachment was over.

Brice had many homes—two up in the mountains—one in Maine, a lake cabin in Alaska. And according to Tally's research he spent a lot of time traveling to them.

But his hub of operations—the political work he did—was out of a house in Aurora, Colorado, a suburb of Denver. He built a large house on four city lots and fenced it all with cedar planking and played the life of a rich—incredibly rich—suburban dweller. At least on the outside. The house had all the latest security systems—à la Ollie North—and he was seldom alone. Neighbors spoke of comings and goings in the night and tall men with straight backs and boxes. Brice had stated that he felt he needed to be close to Denver, to his operations and there was probably some truth to that.

Tally knew he was there now. Or was probably there.

And he was probably not alone.

It didn't make any difference. Tally was going straight in.

He pulled into the driveway and stopped the Jeep, got out. The house was lighted from the outside but seemed to be dark on the inside.

He felt at his back and took the automatic out, held it down alongside his leg, walked to the front door and leaned on the bell.

At some length he heard footsteps and was surprised when the man who opened the door—fully clothed—was Brice Devon himself.

"Yes." He was tall, assured, cold. "What do you want?"

"Here's how it works," Tally said. "You fucked up and I'm going to tear you down for it. You shouldn't have gone after Kari. . . ."

"I don't have any idea what you're talking about."

"Right. I understand." Now that he was doing it Tally could not believe the anger he felt; not just anger, but rage. An exultant, wild rage. His voice was trembling with it, his hand in back of his leg holding the automatic shook with it, his whole body was alive with it. "I just want you to know that I am not the police and I will not stop. Not until you are shit. Do you understand?"

Brice smiled—a tight movement of his lips. "There is nothing to understand. Normally I let Howard handle these things for me." He pulled the door further open and Tally saw another man standing there.

He was dressed in pants and tennis shoes, obviously thrown on rapidly, and a tee shirt. He was holding a gun, a revolver. Tally knew he was the man. The man Brice had sent to Kari and something clicked in him, almost an audible click and he was past any kind of normal control.

He stepped forward in one swift movement and brought his hand around from in back of his leg, raised the automatic and put the barrel exactly in the nostril of the man.

Howard.

There was not time for any reaction, no stopping it. Even Tally was not ready for it, hadn't shown any indication that he was going to move.

"The gun. Hand me the gun." Tally's voice was flat. "With your thumb and finger."

Howard brought the gun up and forward, pinching it between his thumb and forefinger. Tally took it with his left hand and dropped it on the floor.

Still holding the automatic on Howard he backed half a step and with a short left cross caught Brice full on in the face with his fist in a flat line, knuckles straight across the bridge of Brice's nose.

It was a professional blow. There were years of

experience in back of it; starting as a fighter in the marines, where he was division champion, through all the years of kicking around, fighting in bars and dumps all over the world.

A mean punch and he felt/heard Brice's nose crumple into mush as the man went down.

All of this in seconds, two or three at the most, and he turned back to Howard.

"If you move I will kill you."

Howard said nothing, had said nothing and held the silence now while Tally hit him. Higher this time, across the eyes and forehead so the man's head snapped back. He was a fighter, had probably been Green Beret, but the blow came so fast and so hard he had no time to react. His eyes came up, crossed—seemed to want to stare at the point of impact—and he started down as well, back against the wall and sliding down.

Tally did not stop.

He could not stop.

He hit the man twice more as he was on the way down; calculated blows, aimed into the center of Howard's face but going for a point about a foot in back of Howard's head.

He heard his own knuckles crack and knew that something had broken. It didn't matter. With Howard down he changed hands on the automatic, held it in his broken left hand and used his right hand to hit him four more times, Howard's head bouncing back off the wall with each jar, slamming back and bouncing loosely forward.

His face was gone, mush, and Tally knew that part of it was driven back into his skull and still he did not stop until Howard was completely loose, until there was nothing left to the man.

Then he stood away and up and took a breath, his hands hanging at his sides, blood dripping from them, the automatic held by the back of the receiver and he thought clinically that he'd been using a bit too much lower arm in the blows.

Should have carried more shoulder down into them, he thought; that always was my weakness. Too much clubbing, not enough depth. Needed more shoulder and a little cleaner delivery.

He walked back to the Jeep. He tried to fit the automatic back into the holster at his back but his hands were already swelling and didn't seem to want to work very well. Finally he threw it on the passenger seat and climbed in.

Too much lower arm.

That was the trouble.

He started driving back to the hospital to check on Kari again. His movements awkward and clumsy on the wheel. They could tape his hands up there and he'd sit with her until morning.

Then he saw that there was light coming to the sky over the eastern prairie and turned to see the gold of morning catching the tops of the mountains and knew that it was already morning.

He did not know that he was crying, and had been for some time; for all the time that he was beating Howard and Brice down he'd been crying silently and still was, the tears making lines on his cheeks but he knew nothing of it.

CHAPTER TWENTY-NINE

DAVEY HAD WORKED out a plan.

It seemed like they flew for hours and hours and he wondered for awhile if they were ever going to come down but he was glad because it gave him time to work out a plan.

It was simple.

He would pretend to be drugged and when the plane landed as soon as the pilot opened the door he would jump and run. He did not know where they were or where they were flying except he saw lights and knew it would not be over the ocean.

But the lights were coming farther and farther apart and he guessed that must mean they were flying over the desert but it didn't matter.

First he had to get away, to run. And that was as far as his plan went. Pretend to be drugged and run like old billy hell when he got a chance. Run and don't look back.

The first part went well.

The plane kept roaring through the sky and every time the pilot looked back at him Davey made sure he was looking out the window and grinning and he even let his head wobble a little bit and acted screwy. Once he raised his hands and laughed and that time the pilot looked at him strangely so he decided to not make such a thing of it and held back a little.

But it worked.

The pilot pretty much ignored him and when they had been flying for what seemed like days the pilot spoke in the radio to somebody who answered him, then reached out to the dashboard and started doing things with the controls and the engine cut back, hardly making any sound and the plane started down. There was a bump and two large panels stuck down in back of the wing just over Davey's head and the plane slowed still more and seemed to swim down, wobbling around, down into the darkness.

There were no lights where they were going down, not a one below them and the pilot brought the plane around in shallow circles as he let the plane sink.

Then Davey saw it, one bright light. It flashed once, down a bit and out to the side and after it flashed Davey could see that it was another plane.

The pilot flipped some switches and there was another flash of light, bright as day and on and off around the plane—Davey knew that he had turned his landing lights on and off from movies he'd seen on television—and the pilot seemed to tip the plane on its side and it slid down towards the ground.

The sudden move scared Davey and he caught his breath and wanted to yell but before anything came out the pilot had flattened the plane and turned the landing lights on and was settling the plane onto a dirt strip. There were some bumps but not too bad and the pilot steered the plane to the end of the runway and turned it around with some gunning of the engine and then turned the light off.

They waited only a moment and then Davey saw the other plane flash its lights and come in to land and he saw that it had two engines and was bigger than the plane he was in but seemed to land just as easily and he thought all this for me? Two planes just to move one kid around?

But there wasn't time now for thinking. The two-engine plane moved close to them and wheeled around with its engines throwing up clouds of dust and sand.

It stopped and two men got out, stepped on the wing and down to the ground and started walking towards the plane Davey was in.

Nothing was working right.

The pilot didn't reach around to loosen his belt or open the door but just sat in the front, waiting for the two men to come to the plane.

There would not be a chance to get away. They would open the door and be right there and he would not have a chance and he knew that if it was going to happen, if he was going to run, he would have to make the move now.

Right now.

He unhooked the seat belt, took a deep breath and leaned forward in the seat and reached for the door handle.

"What the hell?"

The pilot turned and it was all in slow motion for Davey. The pilot turned and saw him reaching for the handle on the small door just as Davey grabbed it, pulled it down and the door came loose.

He jumped forward, felt the pilot grab his arm, felt his hand hard and strong holding him and knew there was not a way he could escape, felt the same sick fear he'd felt when the big man named Rev had grabbed him and held him.

He started to fall back, to give up. His legs seemed to cave in and he thought that it wasn't fair, that he hadn't even come close when there was a flash of light to the side of the runway and he saw a hole appear in the windshield of the airplane just in front of the pilot and the pilot slammed back in the seat and let go of Davey's arm.

Over the sound of the engine Davey heard the crack of a gun, a big gun—all at the same time, in the same instant. The flash, the hole in the windshield and the pilot falling back and the sound and he had only part of a second to wonder before he realized he was being given a second chance.

He grabbed the door handle, jerked it, lunged forward and fell out on the ground.

CHAPTER THIRTY

Martin worked the bolt smoothly, the pain in his hands forgotten now that things had started.

The first plane had landed and he saw that the second was coming in so he had waited for it. They had radios he knew and he thought that if he shot the first plane on the ground the pilot would tell the second plane and it would not land.

So he had waited until they were both on the ground and near where he lay at the end of the runway and two men had gotten out of the big plane before opening fire.

It was hard to shoot at night. He had forgotten how difficult the darkness made it and he shot high on the first shot. He had aimed at the engine of the small plane with the first round thinking that one bullet would be enough to stop it but the bullet had gone high and he saw that it took the windshield.

But he worked the bolt well and held the barrel down a bit and the second bullet went into the engine. There was a small cloud of smoke that went back, blown by the propellor and the engine made a whining sound and stopped, kicking over twice or three times but Martin did not hear it.

Two bullets had gone out of the rifle and that meant he had three more before he had to reload.

He brought the barrel to the left and hit the right engine on the larger plane and this time there was smoke and some flames flickered in the prop wind.

One more, he thought. One more just to make certain but he knew he didn't have to shoot the plane again. The flames grew and worked back on the engine until the wing itself seemed to be burning and Martin had pride that he had done it.

In three shots from the rifle he had kept both planes on the ground.

But there was not time to think. Much was happening.

The two men had stopped between the planes, frozen with the suddenness of Martin's shooting. One of them—the larger of the two men—pulled a gun out and fired at Martin but it was not much of a gun, one of the small pistols, and it made only a small sound and the bullets went well over Martin's head. Stupid, he thought, to shoot that way. . . .

Then a smaller figure—he thought at first it must be a woman—jumped from the first plane and dropped to the ground and started to run. In the light from the burning wing on the larger plane Martin saw that it was not a woman but a boy, a small boy, and he wondered how it could be that a boy was involved in this thing with the drugs and who would be so stupid as to bring a child?

But there was other more urgent work. He moved the bolt again. Two more bullets left—two more in the magazine. Carlos would have been proud. He had always been angered by the price of bullets and he would bc proud to see Martin doing so well with so few bullets.

The man with the small gun fired another time at Martin and this time held the small gun right and Martin felt a stinging on the side of his left arm where it went up to the stock of the rifle. But it was not much of a sting, not much of a hit and he started to shoot the man.

Then the large man did a strange thing.

Rather than shoot at Martin again he turned the

small gun on the man next to him, put it to his head and there was a small popping sound and the man went down as sheep went down when they were shot for butchering. His legs were not there and he went down and Martin thought again, how strange that was—why would he do that?

He decided he would not kill the big man because he wished to ask him why he shot the other man. So he held the rifle low and shot the big man through the legs. The bullet meant for bear hit the man in the left knee and the knee exploded in a spray of bone and the leg flew out to the side and he fell to the ground, the small gun spinning out and away and Martin worked the bolt again.

One bullet left.

The plane with two engines exploded while the pilot was trying to get out of the door completely covering him in flames and he dropped back into the inferno as if shot. The wounded man on the ground began to drag himself along the sand, moving away from the heat of the fire and Martin heard the small voice for the first time.

"Help," the little voice said. "Help me."

And he turned to see the boy standing there, crying, lighted by the flames from the plane, tears running down his cheeks and one hand raised so that he looked like the supplicating Christ in the church in Tres Piños.

"Please help me."

CHAPTER THIRTY-ONE

TALLY STARED AT the piece of paper in the Olivetti.

White, clean, blank.

The story.

He felt the old excitement that came with knowing the story would be good, could work, would work. The tightness in his stomach, the hairs going up on the back of his neck—the quickening, he thought. The Moment.

It had all happened, all come together.

Tyron had called him at six in the morning at the hospital.

"You awake?"

"Yes." Tally had not slept, had not closed his eyes; had been sitting watching Kari sleep, not thinking, not knowing anything. He had not even felt the nurse taping his knuckles.

"You won't believe this—some old shit with a First World War rifle started a war down in New Mexico last night. He thought it was a drug drop and he shot hell out of these two airplanes."

"Christ."

"Exactly. There were only two survivors. One of the perps with his leg about blown off and—God, I love this—a small boy who had been kidnapped in San Diego about a week and a half ago. . . ."

"We've got to get down there."

"I know. I can't go officially. The feds got it but I applied for a leave of absence effective immediately and reserved two seats on the seven o'clock flight to Albuquerque. Meet me at Stapleton. . . ."

And it had all unraveled.

It was a classic, really, Tally thought, looking at the blank paper. A classic story.

The boy had proven to be smart and had an excellent memory. He named the man in San Diego and the feds got the bastard along with some nurse who worked with him. They in turn identified some guy in Los Angeles who in turn gave a solid make on the man who had been shot in the leg. He had copped out and identified not just the man he had killed but another man—apparently the linch pin of the whole operation—some guy in Boston named Rissden.

There was one bad spot. They would not get Brice Devon or apparently any of the other "customers." Not unless Rissden named them. He was the only link. So the true, miserable sons of bitches—the true scum—were safe. Although the feds had a good case against Rissden and he might want to bargain later.

An operation—a goddamn business. A catering service for private parties.

Tally had spent the last month living on airplanes, flying from Los Angeles to San Diego to Albuquerque to Denver to Boston and back again.

"Children," he typed, "have always been the primary victims. In Victorian England they were bought and sold almost on open market when it was thought that the only cure for syphilis—a disease which riddled the upper classes—was to make love to a young virgin. . . ."

No. He pulled the paper out and stuck a new piece in. That had to be in there, but later. The story didn't start there. It didn't start with sex or children.

Where? Further back? All the way back when Herod slaughtered the Innocents on the night he thought Christ was born? When Abraham was willing to sacrifice his son to some misbegotten image of God?

No. New paper. Blank, white. Clean. Honest. You couldn't lie to the paper. It didn't start earlier, it started later. Much later.

The story started not with a beginning but with an end, with how it stopped—as all stories did. And it stopped because of one old man who was trying to get some pain killer for his arthritis. Luck—it was all luck.

He leaned back, away from the paper because he knew he had it now and didn't have to worry, didn't have to push. He looked at the phone but it was almost automatic. He knew she wouldn't call. He had waited and watched almost constantly for the first two weeks, checking the machine each time he came home but she hadn't called and he knew she wouldn't call and he didn't blame her; knew she was right.

The story was there now.

He almost didn't need all the scraps of paper, notes, tapes that he had made and that were scattered around the living room, on the coffee table, the couch, the kitchen table.

Now it was just typing.

"Martin Flores," he wrote, "waited for seventeen days in the desert. . . ."

The story was there.